Victoria straightened up, prepared for battle

"You said there was something you wanted to discuss with me," she said lightly. She felt trapped, threatened, yet logically she had absolutely no cause to feel guilt. She could feel the tension mounting.

Julius was gazing at her intently, the silver-gray of his eyes unnervingly penetrating, anger evident in every line of his body.

"I realize I was a distance away," he began, his voice suddenly colder. "But Andrew had my telephone number. And my office here could have contacted me."

She kept her eyes fixed on the carpet in front of the fireplace. She didn't move. She couldn't.

"Why didn't you tell me about the baby, Victoria?"

Rosalie Ash, an English writer, abandoned her first intended career for marriage, then worked as a personal secretary for the managing director of a group of building and leisure companies. She stopped work to have her first child and now has two daughters. Somehow during the hectic days and broken nights, first days at school and ferrying to and from various lessons, Brownies and so on, her new writing career emerged. After a lifelong compulsion to write—and numerous secret scribblings—she finally achieved her ambition to write romance novels. Other pleasures she and her family enjoy are regular visits to the Royal Shakespeare Theatre, entertaining friends, country walks, reading, films and travel.

Melting Ice

Rosalie Ash

Harlequin Books

TORONTO • NEW YORK • LONDON
AMSTERDAM • PARIS • SYDNEY • HAMBURG
STOCKHOLM • ATHENS • TOKYO • MILAN

Original hardcover edition published in 1989
by Mills & Boon Limited

ISBN 0-373-17055-6

Harlequin Romance first edition February 1990

CHAPTER ONE

'EIGHTEEN . . . nineteen . . . twenty!' Victoria gasped, finally relaxing the tension in her arms and lowering her legs back down to the ground. She sank back on her heels on the spongy cushion of pine needles and assessed the distance she had covered. Ten feet this time. Not bad at all, considering it was a year since she'd walked on her hands. She had usually won the competitions on the school playing-field, and it was satisfying to know the intervening twelve months at university hadn't dimmed her expertise.

With long, rather grubby fingers she thrust the unruly red curls back from her forehead and glanced round her. It had just occurred to her how infantile she might look to anyone watching, but she shrugged that thought away. This was Great Heath Copse, one of the least frequented corners of her father's eight-hundred-acre farm, and the chances of anyone observing her, even the farmhands operating the combine harvesters on the barley in Lower Cowdown, were slight.

Besides, what did it matter? Walking on her hands was admittedly a rather silly, childish pastime, but somehow it fitted her mood today. Just because she had completed a year of a degree course, she didn't have to turn studious and sedate, did she? Stretching slender, expressive arms up towards the glorious September sun, she felt a surge of pure joy to be alive, and happy to be home.

This secluded copse of pines was a childhood haunt. It bordered the river, and there was an old wooden seat

she had made herself, years ago, from a plank and two
wooden blocks, which caught the afternoon sun through
the trees. She used to come here after school, sometimes
with Hayley, until her older sister grew too grand for such
bucolic delights, sometimes with a friend from school, but
mainly alone, with her homework and a picnic hastily
grabbed from the hubbub of the farmhouse kitchen.

Screwing up her eyes now at the sun, she tried to assess
the time by its position. She'd forgotten to put on her
watch this morning, in the breakfast-time scramble with
Hayley and baby William, but it was probably getting on
for six o'clock. She ought to get back. She had strolled
over here almost two hours ago, bringing a steak pie for
her father as a good excuse to spend a nostalgic afternoon
revisiting all her old haunts, but Hayley would probably
appreciate some help with William while she prepared
dinner.

But she just had time for one more go on her hands. See
if she could get up to twenty-five. Skilfully inverting
herself once more, she began counting again, reaching
fifteen before she heard the deep murmur of men's voices
approaching, and before she had time to lower herself
gracefully down, a pair of elegant grey leather shoes, now
coated with the dark brown mud peculiar to this part of
central England, were planted squarely in her path. With
commendable balance, she tipped her chin towards her
chest and peered up through her arms. Above the grey
shoes stretched a long, muscular body, in an expensive
charcoal-grey suit, a blur of navy and white striped shirt,
dark face and short-cropped, silvery-blond hair. Victoria
wobbled precariously.

'Will you get out of my way, please?' she gasped, with
difficulty. 'You're right in my way. That's the way I
come down.'

The elegantly muddy shoes stepped out of vision, but

by now she knew it was too late to make a controlled descent. She was falling over backwards. Intending to lower herself into a forward somersault, she completely lost control and instead crash-landed on her back in a clumsy sprawl on the peaty ground.

Her father, grey hair untidy and grinning broadly in his usual ancient brown overalls and mud-plastered green wellingtons, came to haul her up, but she flapped him airily away, winded but gasping with laughter.

'No—I'm OK. Let me get my breath back first.'

'I thought I'd find you here. So this is what you call quiet studying?'

Her father winked at his companion, who was standing motionless at his side. The man's pale eyes were amused as they flicked assessingly over her, and then as she began to struggle to her feet he surprised her by coming to squat on his haunches beside her, and taking her arm in a cool firm grip helped her up, demonstrating impressively strong thigh muscles in the easy, athletic movement.

'You're not hurt?'

She shook her head, momentarily confused by the probing directness of the man's gaze.

'No, no, I don't think so. Thanks to these pine needles, they make a soft landing!' she grinned, shrugging her arm away quickly from his grasp as soon as she was safely upright. His touch had sent a shivery sensation along her nerve ends.

'As you've probably gathered, Julius, this is my younger daughter Victoria.' Her father touched her shoulder lightly as he spoke, adding, 'And this is Julius Korda, Victoria. He's been pricing some of your mother's bits and pieces.'

'Oh, yes.' She focused large brown eyes on the tall blond man, trying to decide why she found him curiously unsettling. So this was Julius Korda, the top London antiques and art expert Andrew had put Dad in touch with. Her brother-in-law had spoken of him with the slightly awed respect he reserved for people who rose from nowhere to self-made success. But maybe he was the kind of man who inspired respect in any case, for more personal reasons, thought Victoria, shivering involuntarily under that laser-sharp stare.

Julius Korda made her feel vulnerable. She wasn't used to feeling vulnerable with men.

'How do you do, Mr Korda?' she said solemnly, holding out a grimy hand with commendable poise. 'Did you discover some priceless piece of Ming being used as the cat's bowl or something?'

With a fleeting glimpse of amusement in his mask-like face, he shook his head slowly. 'No. Besides, everything has a price, Miss Francis.' His voice was deep and clipped. The accent slightly flat, not London exactly, but not Oxford either.

His hand was lean and brown, and his grip firm. Victoria felt a ripple of apprehension as he clasped her hand.

'Julius thinks one or two pieces might fetch a decent price,' her father was saying blandly. 'But you'll have to come over again with Hayley, and check there's nothing your mother wanted you to keep. I don't want to upset you two girls by flogging all the best Urquhart heirlooms.'

'Right, of course.' Victoria felt awkward. She wanted to say it was a pity her father had to 'flog' any of Mother's treasures, that it was a shame he couldn't just get on with running the farm and pay off his turf accountant once and for all. But even with her habit of blunt speaking, she quaked at going quite that far. Instead, she gave her father a quick, impulsive hug, and kissed him on the cheek, feeling him stiffen as he usually did when he was embarrassed by her fierce displays of affection.

'Sorry, Dad. Were you looking for me specially?' she asked, feeling a stab of guilt.

'Well, I was—but I've been showing Julius over the farm as well,' her father said gruffly, his rather bloodshot blue eyes amused in his craggy, weatherbeaten face. 'Hayley rang to see where you'd got to. I dare say she wants to know what time to get dinner.'

'Oh, golly! I'd better get back. Listen, are you *sure* you don't mind me staying with Hayley and Andrew?' she asked anxiously, searching his face for any sign that he needed her, just for some company, or a shoulder to cry on. But he was shaking his head, his eyes unreadable again.

'You're more use to Hayley,' he told her, not unkindly, adding, 'There's a bit of life there as well, you don't want to rattle around in that great draughty farmhouse with just me for company.'

'Oh, Dad! You know I'd love to come home more than——'

'No. I'm better on my own these days.' Her father seemed aware that he had snapped rather abruptly, and his face softened a fraction but not enough to show he'd changed his mind. 'If I feel like getting maudlin, or just plain drunk, I don't want you fussing around me like a little red hen,' he said, ruffling her Titian curls with a rare glimpse of affection. 'Get back to Hayley, and give some of those lovelorn young men a ring! They've been jamming the line since you got back from your jaunt around Europe, Hayley tells me.'

Not considering this worth a reply, she bent to retrieve her bag of books from the makeshift bench, hiding her hurt feelings with a bright smile as she straightened up.

'OK, I'll wander back—and don't forget to heat up that steak pie I brought from Hayley—she said to tell you if you leave it sitting round the kitchen for a week like the last one, she won't cook you any more!'

'I'll have it tonight,' her father promised solemnly, humouring her. 'And you don't need to walk back, Mr Korda here will give you a lift. He's seen enough worthless bits of junk for one day, haven't you?'

'I'd like to come back tomorrow morning and have a closer look at some of the pieces,' Julius said politely as the three of them strolled back, out of the pine copse, alongside waist-high golden corn three-quarters cut now, and then through a lumpy grass meadow where a herd of fat black and white Friesians eyed them placidly as they passed.

Victoria let the men walk ahead, and thoughtfully observed the lean width of Julius Korda's shoulders, through the immaculate cut of his suit jacket, and the easy, rangy way he moved. Like a big cat, he had a loose-limbed, prowling sort of walk. Even four paces behind him, she could feel a fine, indistinct thread of tension unravelling in the air around them. She wondered if she was imagining things. There was a fairy-tale sort of stillness about the mellow autumn afternoon, and the splendour of the open countryside around them. Maybe she was daydreaming this strange, unsettling vibration between herself and Julius Korda.

A sleek black XJS stood amongst the battered, mud-coated machinery and Land Rovers in the farmyard, looking almost as incongruous as Julius Korda's smart shoes and Savile Row suit against her father's ancient wellingtons and torn overalls.

In polite silence, Julius held open the passenger door for her, and then, amid a scattering of clucking hens and wildly barking dogs, the XJS purred out of the yard and bumped down the long, pot-holed lane.

The unnerving silence continued for several minutes until Victoria felt desperately impelled to break it.

'This *is* kind of you,' she heard herself enthusing gauchely. 'Although in fact it's almost as quick to walk across the fields to Hayley's. This road winds backwards and forwards so much.'

Julius nodded but didn't reply, and a quick nervous glance at his profile showed he was looking remote, as if his thoughts were elsewhere. Probably calculating the value of her family's private possessions, thought Victoria resentfully. Then she chided herself. That was unfair. Julius Korda was doing his job, doing what Andrew and her father had invited him here for. If she didn't like it, she supposed it was because she was an incurable romantic who believed everything should stay the same as it always had. Which wasn't possible, she knew.

She glanced at him again. It was hardly Julius Korda's fault if her father was intent on drinking himself to death at the same time as gambling away the farm's profits, was it? She gnawed her lip, her resentment refusing to go away, and finally was sufficiently honest with herself to admit that her resentment stemmed from being completely ignored. This man had a patronising air of detachment, maybe not deliberate, but nevertheless extremely insulting. After all, she told herself fiercely, she hardly expected every man she met to fall to his knees in blind adoration, but she did appreciate a civil interest, some acknowledgement of her existence as a fellow member of the human race. Sitting here beside this man was like sitting next to a robot!

'So you deal in antiques? Where do you operate from?' she asked lightly, to break the uneasy silence.

'London—New York . . .'

'Oh, so you ship antiques out to New York from this country.'

'We have offices in those places. We ship all over the world.'

'And you live in London?' she persevered.

'Yes.'

'But you're not driving back there tonight?' She flashed him her friendliest smile, thinking of his mention of returning to the farm in the morning.

'No. I'm staying with Hayley and Andrew for the weekend,' he said expressionlessly, pulling into the sweeping drive in front of Hayley's long Elizabethan thatched cottage. For some reason, Victoria's heart seemed to plummet in dismay at the prospect of having Julius Korda for a fellow weekend guest. Maybe it was beause his attitude conveyed a distinct lack of enthusiasm on the same subject!

'Oh, that's nice,' she heard herself babbling idiotically, her usually light rapid speech accentuated through slight nervousness. 'You've probably gathered I'm staying here too . . .'

Julius cut the ignition and turned strange, silver-grey eyes on her, studying her confusion with a detached amusement. Although he appeared far too polite, and presumably uninterested, to allow his gaze to roam down over the silhouette of her figure beneath her baggy green T-shirt and denim bermudas, his inspection still made her painfully self-conscious, body-conscious. She was aware of her lack of make-up, her hastily tied ponytail and grimy knees and hands. She felt like a grubby schoolgirl under that cool scrutiny, or worse still like a specimen on a laboratory table, being mentally dissected.

'Yes, I did gather that!' he said, with a glint of mockery in his eyes.

It took quite a lot to make Victoria annoyed, and she rarely took an instant dislike to people, particularly on first acquaintance. But this man's condescending attitude was really getting under her skin.

Turning abruptly away, she scrambled out of the car as

quickly as she could and walked away from him, without looking round, aware that he was following her as she went round the side of the cottage to the back garden.

She was saved further efforts at communication by the chaos which met them as they reached the terrace.

Hayley had brought William's high chair out into the evening sun to give him tea, and as she rose to greet them William quickly took advantage of the diversion to up-end his bowl of mashed banana over his head, chuckling with glee.

'Here, give him to me,' Victoria offered, glad of something practical to do, darting with him into the kitchen to sponge the food from William's wispy red hair while Hayley produced wine and glasses. 'Come on, sunbeam, Auntie Victoria will take charge of you now. We're kindred spirits, aren't we, Wills?'

'Well, careful, he'll only twist your nose and pull your hair,' Hayley laughed, as they emerged on to the terrace again and she proceeded to pour generous splashes of Andrew's best white Bordeaux into three glasses. 'There—I'm always nervous of serving wine to you, Julius. You hardly ever drink, do you, and when you do, you only drink the best, I seem to remember! Is it a good wine, do you think?'

'I'll give you my verdict in a minute,' Julius murmured drily.

Victoria risked studying him under her thick, gold-brown lashes, wondering caustically if he ever actually smiled properly, and how nice he might look if he did. She really ought to suggest it to him. Anything which dispelled that arctic chill from his features would be an improvement, if only a slight one.

She met his eyes then, that arrogant, penetrating gaze, and looked away quickly. Her breath suddenly felt constricted in her throat, and her mouth had become uncomfortably dry. She took a gulp of wine, and concentrated on William's antics on her lap.

'Ouch, that hurts, young man,' she remonstrated, carefully disentangling his sticky fingers from her long red ponytail. 'Don't pull hair!'

'Dopple hair!' William announced proudly, and repeated it several times as he tried to grab another handful. Laughingly holding her riotous curls on top of her head, out of reach, Victoria raised an eyebrow at her elder sister.

'Did you hear that? This baby is going to be a genius!'

'Hmmm. A genius or a master criminal,' Hayley pronounced, eyeing her son with a wry tolerance. 'Look at him—"Just William" sums him up. He's even getting freckles!'

'Where from, I wonder?' Victoria mused, extending a long, creamy arm, tanned a smooth pale shade of tea from her summer spent roaming the Continent with a group of student friends. She compared it with Hayley's identical skin. 'We might be redheads, but we don't suffer from red-headed skin!'

'We've got Mother's skin, that's why. There was a romantic hint of illicit Spanish somewhere back along the Urquhart line, I believe, wasn't there? Didn't Great-Great-Great-Grandfather do something shocking with a Spanish *señorita*?'

'Goodness knows! I'm studying history, not genealogy. I think you just made that up!'

'No, honestly. I've always thought that's where you get your Gallic arm movements from—it's your Spanish ancestry coming out!'

'What absolute rubbish!' said Victoria, bursting out laughing. 'And anyway, that doesn't explain where William gets his freckles.'

'From Andrew—don't tell me you've never noticed

your brother-in-law has freckles?' Hayley laughed
teasingly, then turned to Julius with eyebrows raised.
'Well? What's the verdict on the wine? I'm sure you
wouldn't be so rude as to say it's frightful, anyway. It's
one of Andy's prize vintages.'

'A very good wine,' he pronounced smoothly.

'That's a relief!'

Victoria was fascinated to watch Hayley's efforts to
thaw their guest, and the degree of success as Julius
Korda appeared to melt a fraction under the dazzling
smile, the slanted brown eyes dancing in Hayley's
beautiful, high-cheekboned face as she tossed her long,
red-gold hair in the sunlight. This, Victoria realised, was
a new role her sister enjoyed playing since she stopped
work to have William. The decorative, gracious, perfect
wife and mother, cleverly hiding one of the sharpest
brains on the Stock Exchange, with a membership of
Mensa and her last earnings approaching the supertax
bracket.

She reflected how different they were. Not physically,
of course. Physically they were almost mirror-images,
both taking after the Urquhart side, apart from her own
red-gold hair curling in a long, unruly cloud round her
shoulders and down her back, whereas Hayley's hung
stick-straight and enviably glossy and smooth.

But their personalities were very different. Just as
Hayley's hair was smooth and glossy, so her sister's
manner had matured to a sophisticated competence. She
couldn't imagine ever being as poised and serene as
Hayley.

She cuddled William thoughtfully, only half listening to
the conversation between her sister and Julius Korda,
until she realised suddenly that Hayley had asked her
something and was waiting patiently for an answer.

'I'm sorry—what did you say?'

'I said, how was Dad?'

'Oh, the same. He's really missing Mum, I think. But he promised to eat that pie tonight.'

'I sent Julius straight over when he arrived, because I knew you'd still be there, and really I don't think Dad's got a clue what there is in the house! Did you show Julius where everything was?'

Victoria looked guilty. 'I must admit I'd disappeared down to my old spot by the river with some books,' she explained awkwardly. 'I—er—I was doing some important revision when Dad and Mr Korda found me!'

She grinned involuntarily at Julius, trying to quell her earlier resentment. If he was staying here for the weekend, she could hardly maintain a sulky silence towards him all the time. Besides, sulking wasn't in her nature.

Seeing Hayley's raised eyebrows, Julius said, 'Victoria appeared to be rehearsing a very impressive circus act.'

Hayley chuckled. 'Oh, say no more. I expect she was walking on her hands—correct?'

Victoria nodded, and Hayley laughed. 'You'd be surprised to learn that she's actually a lot more grown-up than she looks! More wine, Julius?'

'Not for me. If you don't mind, I'd like to take a shower—it was a long, hot drive down from London this afternoon.'

'Of course! How rude of me, packing you straight off to the farm the moment you arrived!' Hayley exclaimed, leaping up and waving to him to follow her into the house. 'Come on, I'll show you your room, and at least I can tell you you've got your own private bathroom! Bring your suitcase up.'

By the time her sister had returned, Victoria had put William into his playpen in the big beamed kitchen, and was stacking his tea things into the dishwasher.

Hayley closed the door behind her, looking thoughtful, almost preoccupied, and when she had poured them both more wine she washed her hands, donned an enormous yellow apron and busied herself boning two pheasants she had cooked the night before. Victoria tackled a pile of potatoes, scrubbing them vigorously under the cold tap, and casting curious glances at her sister. She had half expected Hayley to launch into an enjoyable gossip about their weekend visitor, and when she stayed silent she suddenly wondered if she was thinking the same rather forlorn thoughts she'd been thinking, about Mother's death from cancer last year, and how awful it seemed for Father to be planning to sell any of her precious things from the farm. Although the farm itself had been in Dad's family for generations, her mother had been from an old, county family, and most of the furniture and ornaments in the farmhouse had been hers. The Urquharts seemed to be an endless source of silver, antiques, pictures and porcelain, hence Dad's brainwave of raising money for the farm now that Mum had gone.

Finding it hard to put her own thoughts into words, for fear of sounding petty-minded, or, worse still, covetous of the treasures for herself, she decided it was safer not to talk about that with Hayley. Instead, she grinned at the pheasants her sister was struggling with, greasy-fingered, the pile of fiddly small bones scattered over the huge scrubbed table.

'That smells wonderful!' she sighed, sniffing the tantalising savoury aroma in the air. 'Don't tell me its good for us as well! Or have you abandoned the health kick?'

'Not at all! Game is low-fat, low-calorie—very healthy indeed,' laughed her sister good-naturedly. 'We're getting crankier by the day, of course! Less salt, less sugar, less fat, more fibre. The model family.'

'Very commendable! If you weren't a dairy farmer's daughter! In the circumstances, I don't know how you dare,' Victoria pointed out, eyeing the tub of margarine on the table.

'When you've a little infant of your own to bring up, you'll be just as fanatical as me about the right diet, so stop sneering!'

'I wasn't! But I've no plans to have any little infants of my own in the foreseeable future. Do you want these courgettes scrubbing too?'

'Please, love. But not too hard—you'll damage the skins. And stick those potatoes on skewers, will you? They'll cook quicker. I pre-cooked this casserole yesterday, so when I've dug out all the bones I've only got to heat it up again for an hour or so and, *voilà*! Pheasant *forestière à la* Mackenzie household!'

They worked in silence again, while William sat quietly for once in his playpen, absorbed in balancing a third brick on top of his tower, almost cross-eyed in the process, showing every sign of inheriting Hayley's sharp, mathematical brain, Victoria thought fondly. The only sound apart from William's laboured breathing was the whirring of the wall-clock above the Aga, and finally Victoria could stand the suspense no longer.

'All right. If you won't volunteer the information, I suppose I'll have to be nosey about Julius Korda. You might have warned me you were inviting him this weekend!'

'Ah, I wondered when you'd admit how interested you are in him,' Hayley chuckled, expertly sliding the boned pheasant into its rich red wine sauce, and scraping the skin and bones into the bin. She put the casserole into the Aga, and began to peel some cooking apples.

'He is rather gorgeous, isn'the? I always think men with those sort of half-hooded eyes look as if they're inviting you to bed with them all the time, but Julius is so—sort of deliciously detached. All steely reserve and repressed passion.' Hayley gave an enjoyably exaggerated shiver, and Victoria threw up her hands and glared at her in some annoyance,

'For goodness' sake! I thought you were supposed to be a devoted wife and mother.'

Hayley's brown eyes were dancing. 'I am! That doesn't stop me appreciating another man's—positive characteristics, does it?' She laughed at Victoria's pained expression, and the younger girl realised that she was being well and truly teased. She hunched her shoulders slightly in a casual shrug.

'Well, I'd hardly describe him as gorgeous. I prefer human beings, not robots!'

'Decided that while you were gazing at him longingly on the terrace, did you?'

'I was *not*! If I was gazing at him at all, I was thinking what a granite-faced automaton he looks!' she exclaimed heatedly, incensed by the injustice. Hayley laughed again.

'The lady doth protest too much methinks,' she needled.

Victoria threw a lump of courgette at her in mock rage, then saw William's interested face and clapped a hand to her mouth.

'Oops, sorry, bad example,' she said meekly, and Hayley nodded in reproval.

'It certainly is. If he throws bricks at the other children at playgroup I'll have to say his Auntie Victoria taught him all he knows!'

'Well, I'm sorry, but come on, Hayley. I'm just dying of curiosity. I have to admit it!'

'Well, there's not a lot to explain. I couldn't tell you Julius was coming because I didn't know for certain myself. He'd told Andrew he'd get down if he could. The pheasants last night were a hunch, that's all!'

'And how long have you known him?'

'Oh, years. He's an old friend of Andy's through the antique and fine arts side of Andy's estate agency. But it's funny really, Julius is really rather out of our class these days. Financially, I mean.' Hayley stopped slicing apples, her face reflective. 'Put it this way: if you think your brother-in-law does rather well out of his estate agency, you'll be staggered by how well Julius's outfit does out of the antique trade.'

'He sounds like a bit of a wide-boy to me,' Victoria said caustically, and Hayley hooted with laughter.

'Oh, most certainly not. He's a director of a highly respected firm of antique and fine art auctioneers. But there was a time—not too many years ago—when Julius was extremely hard up. He's had an odd, lonely sort of upbringing, I believe, but he never talks about it. That strange colouring has a bit of Danish or Finnish somewhere, according to Andrew, but Julius is terribly non-committal.'

Victoria gave a twist of a smile, thinking about his cool silence during the short drive from the farm, and nodded,

'Yes, I can imagine.'

'Anyway, now he's a top dog in De Lember and Greysteils. They've got showrooms you could park a couple of Concordes in. Strings of companies specialising in this and that. All to do with arts and antiques. Julius is actually their top art and porcelain expert, but really he's incredibly knowledgeable about just about anything you care to name in the antique world. Andrew thought he'd be the person to call in. I mean, apart from knowing far more than Andy does, it would have been too embarrassing for Andy to do it.'

Victoria could see her point. It was far better for a

complete outsider to come in and select some valuable
items worth selling to bale Dad out of his financial
difficulties. Andrew was too close to it all.

'How come you've invited him to stay the weekend?'
she asked her sister curiously. 'I mean, he's hardly a
laugh a minute, is he!'

Hayley looked surprised. 'Julius? He may appear cool,
but he's a very old friend. Both Andy and I are terribly
fond of him. Besides, it's nice to have a visit from
someone who still lives in the Big City.'

'Ah, yes! I'm surprised you haven't gone back to work
by now.'

Hayley's glance was appalled. 'What? Leave little
William to the mercies of a nanny? I don't need to zoom
back to the City to prove I'm an intelligent human being,
you know! Child-rearing is a *very* important job!'

Victoria hastily amended her words. 'I didn't say it
wasn't. All I meant was, I'm surprised *you* prefer being at
home to—to your high-powered world of finance. Are
you really as contented as you seem?'

Hayley sat down and took a sip of wine, her brown eyes
level.

'Yes, I am. I'm surprised you should doubt it. I mean,
Mum and Dad made a pretty good job of home-making
for us, didn't they? Well, I want to re-create it here for
Andrew and William and all the rest of the children I
intend to have!'

Victoria felt a hard lump in her throat, and gave her
sister an impulsive hug. 'And you have already,' she
confirmed warmly, moved by the frank, somehow
vulnerable admission. William was prompted into a chant
of 'Me hug, me hug' until she relented and picked him
up, holding the warm, solid little boy tightly in her arms
and dancing around the kitchen with him until he
squealed with laughter.

'Don't get him too excited, its bedtime. Oh, lord, is that Julius coming back downstairs? Go and talk to him, will you, darling?'

Pulling a face, Victoria tiptoed theatrically to the door and peered round it, finger to her lips.

'It's OK, Andrew's just come in, and he's taking him into the sitting-room.'

'Well, listen, will you get me some of that clotted cream you brought up from Exeter with you out of the freezer? Then go and be sociable with the men while I get on with things.'

'Must I? It seems a shame to leave everything to you.'

'No, that's all right. Sheila's coming in a few minutes. She'll take over down here while I get Wills to bed.'

Briefly glancing at Victoria, she added,

'And for goodness' sake get showered and changed! You look like one of Fagin's urchins in that state.'

'Yes, miss, no, miss.' Victoria mock-saluted as she reached into the freezer for cream, hesitating, a sudden idea forming in her mind.

'Can I raid your wardrobe?'

'Go on, then,' Hayley groaned, and Victoria slipped out into the hall, avoiding the low drone of male voices from the sitting-room and dating swiftly and gracefully upstairs. Fifteen minutes later, she reassessed her appearance in the cheval mirror in Hayley's room. All the grime was showered away, and gone was the leggy waif in T-shirt and shorts, with dusty bare feet and dirt-streaked face. Instead a slender, elegant girl gazed back. No, not a girl, a woman, she told herself firmly. The ivory silk, with its subtle rust stripe, felt sensuous against her skin, and for once she felt *womanly*. Hayley had lovely clothes. She would have to buy herself some more sophisticated things. A wardrobe full of denims and sweatshirts, supplemented by a passion for collecting matching shoes and belts, was fine for the casual atmosphere of the university campus, but sometimes—she chewed her lip, momentarily confused. Was it the silk which had wrought this strange transformation into conscious femininity, or was it the peculiar effect Julius Korda had on her? She mocked herelf. Surely that man's cold lack of interest couldn't possibly have triggered this sudden desire to be appreciated as a woman. That struck her as extremely ironic! But nevertheless, she moved to stand sideways and the full skirt moved softly with her, caressing and swirling around her bare, tanned legs. She and Hayley were the same dress-size, but she was a little better endowed in the bustline—dubiously she eyed the buttons she had left undone on the loose, classic blouse. Just enough to banish the tomboyish little character her father had introduced this afternoon—yes, not bad. A distinct improvement. Maybe a touch of jewellery, nothing too flashy. She searched feverishly in Hayley's china bowl, feeling like some sort of scheming hussy, and already getting an overwhelming desire to dissolve into giggles.

Clipping on discreet gold hoops and matching choker, she tugged her hair loose from its tight ponytail and pulled a brush vigorously through the curls, leaving it cascading in a thick Titian cloak down her shoulders. A touch of pearly rust eye-shadow, and some bronze lip-gloss, was the only make-up she needed with the remnants of her summer tan. As a final inspiration, she grabbed Hayley's perfume atomiser and enveloped herself in a sensuous floral cloud ofAnaïs Anaïs, then, slipping her bare feet into cream, high-heeled court shoes, she sauntered to the landing ready to stroll downstairs.

Half-way down, she was assailed by vague disquiet. She wasn't normally vain or self-conscious. She didn't usually care what people thought of her appearance. They could take her or leave her. So what subtle, insidious vibration of response was making her deliberately dress up for Julius Korda?

Once she'd admitted that she *was* dressing up to impress Julius Korda, she was furious with herself. She was about to turn back upstairs and tear off all the finery and throw on jeans and a jumper when the sitting-room door opened, and Andrew saw her on the stairs.

'Ah, here's Victoria, my favourite sister-in-law!' Andrew called jovially. 'Come and talk to Julius, my dear.' He ushered her into the sitting-room, his blue eyes glinting with amusement as he studied her appearance.

'You're looking very sophisticated, Vicky! I'm finally beginning to understand why these young chaps called Michael and Sebastian keep ringing you up!'

With a slightly embarrassed smile she reached up to kiss his cheek just above his sandy beard. Andrew Mackenzie was a wryly humorous Scot, with a habit of poking fun at life in general, and his wife's younger sister in particular. Victoria was quite used to him, and very fond of him, but even so there were times when she could cheerfully strangle him.

'The way you and my father keep on, you'd think the village was under seige from an invading army of suitors,' she quipped, with just a touch of irritation. 'They're just friends, Andrew. The way Karen and Caroline and Shelley are just friends. We all hitched round Europe together this summer, remember? I think I'd have noticed if there was a "grand romance" in the air.'

Her brother-in-law was about to comment but he caught the warning glimmer in her eyes and decided to stop goading her.

'All right, all right. I'll stop. I gather you and Julius met earlier, over at the farm?'

'Yes, we did.' She finally risked glancing towards the other man, who had risen from a chair by the fireplace when she walked in, and was now standing, leaning against the mantelpiece, tall and self-contained, and curiously motionless. Andrew was talking about the situation at the farm, her father's money troubles and the possibility of selling one or two pieces to tide him over his difficult times, but the conversation seemed to have receded to a far-away murmur, meaningless background noises, and her gaze was locked in that aloof, ice-chip stare which was threatening to rip her composure to shreds.

Andrew handed her a glass of wine and unthinkingly she took a hasty gulp and blinked her attention elsewhere with a huge effort of will power. A log fire was smouldering into life in the inglenook fireplace, and intermittent tongues of flame flickered up from the smoke. She went to sit in the window-seat, and watched the beginnings of the fire.

When Andrew left the room in response to a call from Hayley, she sat stiffly in the silence, suddenly rigidly determined that Julius Korda should make the first attempt at conversation this time. That brief taste of his detached, patronising attitude in the car this afternoon still rankled.

'So,' he said at last, his deep voice sounding slightly amused, 'if I raised my original estimate by about five years, would I be nearer the mark?'

She blinked up at him, confused.

'I beg your pardon?'

'Well, I hate to admit it,' his wide mouth twisted wryly, 'but I'd put you down as about fourteen this afternoon!'

She felt something thaw, just a little, inside her. There was enough self-mockery about his hard voice to make him seem, suddenly, slightly more human. She found she was warming to him. Perhaps he was just terribly shy, she decided. Some men were, and they tended to hide it

behind that kind of cold, macho unfriendliness. Her
naturally friendly instincts began to surface again.

'Well, don't worry! I'm not offended,' she laughed.
'You were probably entitled to the mistake. I'll confess I
was feeling a bit nostalgic down there by the river this
afternoon. There's something rather—repressive—about
being grown-up, isn't there?'

'Is there? I've always thought it was the other way
round,' he said, his tone becoming absent, flat, and
slightly bored again, she thought furiously, hardly
inviting further conversation, let alone polite small talk.

'Oh, really?' She tailed off, as the silence grew between
them again. She found herself remembering Hayley's
remarks about his background. Had he found his
childhood repressive? She tried to imagine a childhood
which wasn't filled with rich, warm security, love and
boundless optimism, as her own had been. Or mostly had
been. Maybe, once or twice, she'd sensed that everything
wasn't quite as cosily reassuring as it appeared on the
surface. But the good times were the ones she recalled,
not the bad. And they had been in the majority, hadn't
they?

She watched Julius's long, brown fingers linked loosely
round his glass of Perrier water, and took another large
gulp of her wine. Hayley was quite right, she found
herself acknowledging. He was incredibly attractive.
Blindingly so. He had changed out of the grey suit, and
now wore white jeans and a grey checked shirt. Casual,
but elegantly tailored. Immaculate. His grooming was
almost as faultless as his self-containment, she decided.

Clearing her throat, she fixed him with a calm, slightly
surprised gaze, making it clear that she expected him to
make some contribution, to break the socially
unacceptable silence. Suddenly he seemed to break out of
his brooding reverie, and with a slight easing back of his

wide shoulders he shot her a rueful look.

'Forgive me,' he said seriously, disarmingly. 'You must think me very tedious company. My mind was far away—on a business problem.' He took a sip of Perrier and levelled his clear grey eyes on her with what she took to be a genuine attempt at interest. She wasn't sure whether to be flattered or insulted at this obvious effort he was making.

'So tell me,' he went on, politely. 'How old *are* you?'

'Nineteen. Well, nearly. In two weeks' time. I'm at university in Exeter, doing history and English.'

'Ah, I see. Perhaps it was the reference to studying which fooled me. I assumed you were on holiday from school.'

'I've just passed my prelims!'

'And you're enjoying it?'

'Very much!' she nodded emphatically, her enthusiasm shining. 'I've always loved history. Maybe I should thank my history mistress at school, Miss Parkinson. She brought it all to life for me.' She moved to the edge of the chair, her face unconsciously glowing with animation as she sought to explain herself. 'I always see it as a very personal subject. All those generations who lived before me, all those roots and rhythms—the pattern of things.' She laughed, suddenly aware of the intent expression on Julius's face and becoming conscious of her runaway tongue. 'Sorry—I expect you think I'm raving mad!'

'No, not at all,' said Julius gravely. 'I don't share your love of the past—at least not in the same sense. But I can see it might provide a sense of continuity.'

'That's it, exactly. Sometimes, I sit alone in a really old building, sometimes in the farmhouse, sometimes even here, and I wait and listen. And I can almost imagine myself blending back into the past, I can feel a sense of life spanning generations——' She stopped again, seeking to express herself better. 'I think it helped me to come to terms with my mother's death. The feeling of continuity, of times before and times still to come.'

She flashed a dazzling, slightly embarrassed smile at Julius, and drained her wine-glass, aware that she was drinking too much yet unable to take a hold on her heady emotions. 'Sorry, I must be boring you rigid, Mr Korda. I do tend to ramble on a bit.'

'No, you're not boring me at all. I'm sorry about your mother, Victoria. It must be hard to lose your mother when you're so young. And please call me Julius. When young girls call me Mr Korda it makes me feel very old,' he added, with a twist of a smile.

'Julius, then,' she grinned at him. 'But I'm not *that* young! Nineteen's well past the age of consent, you know! And I think I've grown up quicker in the last twelve months, going to university and living away from home. I share a house in Exeter with some other students. And then Mum dying . . . that somehow gives you the feeling you've got to cope all on your own.' She tailed off, conscious of sounding morose, and then she smiled at him teasingly, 'But I suppose, compared with me, you *are* very old!' she told him cheekily, and was mortified to see a faint, dark flush of colour in his already dark cheeks. She wished she could bite off her tongue. How unforgivably rude of her. Maybe he had a real hang-up about his age. She eyed him remorsefully. He looked thirty-ish but maybe he was more, and starting to panic about the male menopause or whatever men were supposed to have.

'I'm sorry, I really didn't mean that to sound as rude as it did,' she apologised hastily, watching him in apprehension for signs that she had mortally offended him. 'I'm afraid it's a bad habit of mine, saying things without thinking!'

There was a short silence, after her rush of words, and

then to the complete demolition of her composure Julius laughed.

It was an ice-splintering laugh, crinkling the corners of his eyes, and creasing the hard cynical lines of his cheeks into an almost boyish, wholly appealing grin. She was ensnared by the transformation.

'Now we're quits,' he said, still laughing. 'I thought you were fourteen—you think I'm forty-five?'

'Forty-five? No, absolutely not!' she blurted out, in confusion. 'Really, you don't look a day over twenty-nine.'

'Thirty,' he supplied calmly. 'Nearly old enough to be another generation to you.'

'Hardly!' she giggled. 'Unless eleven years old is the average age to start a family.'

Julius laughed again, and she felt her own smile fading as she gazed at him. She felt captured again by that brilliant smile, and by that intense stare. She wanted to say that, far from looking like a member of another generation, he looked the sort of man schoolgirls pinned in poster-form to their bedroom walls and drooled over at bedtime.

But she refrained from making any more outrageous remarks. She was feeling curiously drawn to him, as if he wasn't a comparative stranger she had met only a couple of hours ago, but someone she had known intimately, someone achingly familiar, from some long ago, half-remembered meeting.

She stared into his eyes for what seemed aeons of time, and gradually saw the amusement fade from his eyes and knew that she was making a complete idiot of herself.

Her pulses seemed to have speeded up to a frantic pounding, and a rush of nameless emotion was affecting her stomach muscles in a warm, cramping longing she had never felt before and didn't fully understand.

'Victoria.' Andrew was bending over her, proffering

more wine, and heedlessly she nodded as he poured more
of the clear, cool liquid into her glass. With another
nervous gulp she tore her eyes from Julius, and tried to
erase the imprint of him in her mind. She lowered her lids
briefly, squeezed her eyes tight shut for a second, but the
image was still there, of laughing eyes growing cooler,
retreating from her, dispassionate and coldly appraising
again as if he had read her mind and strongly disapproved
of her foolish, romantic fantasies.

'Are you all right, Vicky?' Andrew was looking at her
in surprise, and she stood up, forcing a smile, and
nodding brightly.

'Yes, I feel a bit dizzy, that's all. Too much sun this
afternoon, I expect. I think I'll go out on the terrace for a
minute.'

She escaped through the french windows into the cooler
evening air, and tried to drag her shattered nerves
together as a blackbird twittered melodiously from the
apple tree on the lawn.

Something had happened to her just then, as she had
stared into Julius's eyes. It was a thing people didn't do
on casual acquaintance, stare into each other's eyes.
There was something frighteningly revealing about
prolonged eye-contact. She shivered, gazing blindly
across the yellow and russet chrysanthemums bordering
the terrace. She knew now why his eyes were so startling.
The pewter-grey irises were ringed with black, yet flecked
with silver, just like ice-crystals on deep, still water.

And something had happened to her, and she suspected
deep down she might never be quite the same again.
Whether Julius has felt the same unnerving experience,
she couldn't tell. Those magnetic eyes had held
something, some disturbing emotion, for a brief few
seconds, but then they had become shuttered again, too
expressionless to read.

CHAPTER TWO

VICTORIA drank far too much wine at dinner, and found herself falling into a familiar trap. If she was disturbed or nervous about something, she reacted by over-exuberance, and not even intercepting amused glances between Hayley and Andy quelled her extrovert behaviour. She kept them all entertained with anecdotes about her university friends, and her hair-raising adventures on their trek around France, Italy and Spain that summer.

After coffee and liqueurs, she found herself pushing back her chair, standing up a trifle unsteadily, and announcing brightly,

'Let's all go dancing! Let's go to Options! Andy—Julius—you'll take us dancing, won't you?'

Options was, in fact, a rather up-market nightclub catering for all ages, so this suggestion didn't meet with total horror. Hayley stifled what sounded suspiciously like a snort of laughter, but Andy seemed happy to humour her, and half an hour later she was returning, breathless, to their table in the velvet dimness of the nightclub, with her friend Sebastian following her a few seconds afterwards, if possible even more out of breath than she was.

She laughed up at him, taking a gulp of her drink.

'Fantastic, bumping into you here, Vicky!' Sebastian was enthusing, collapsing into a spare chair at their table, his brown hair flopping over his forehead. 'No one else I know dances quite like you!'

'Oh, I practice whenever I can,' she laughed. 'It's good for the figure!' She turned recklessly to catch Julius's eye across the table. An ornate Victorian glass lamp stood in the centre, casting a glow over everyone's faces, making Julius's eyes gleam like a cat's. Even with a quantity of wine inside her, she was finding it uncharacteristically difficult to pluck up courage and ask Julius to dance with her. Her wavering spirits annoyed her. It seemed so ridiculous. This was the only man she had ever met who sent such a shimmer of nervous energy through her, made her shiver all over with wild anticipation. Why did he also have to be the only one who had ever reduced her to such pathetic indecisiveness?

'Come on, Julius,' she risked at last, 'dance with me.' She hoped her light-hearted tone masked her desperate fear of rejection. But Julius leaned back in his chair, the cold silver eyes level on her face, a hint of mockery around his hard mouth.

'I'm far too old to keep up with the sort of gymnastics you were doing,' he said casually, almost off-hand, and he picked up his conversation with Andrew where she had interrupted him, ignoring her crimson face with consummate cruelty.

Victoria sat very still, trying to hide her feelings. It was an annoying peculiarity of hers that whenever she was angry, her hands shook. And being angry at this moment was such an irrational emotion she was determined to repress it. Linking her hands together in her lap, she pressed them together, willing herself not to care. Her palms felt slightly moist, though her throat was dry and tight. She had been put down, she acknowledged, as deftly as if she were a precocious schoolgirl and he the headmaster. Sebastian was chattering away to her, relating his sense of anti-climax since coming back from their carefree holiday, but she was unable to listen properly. She couldn't concentrate at all.

After a while, the music slowed, and Julius glanced across the table, and half rose from his chair. Involuntarily, heart thudding, she found herself rising a little off her own chair, in readiness for his invitation, but belatedly she realised he had raised that eloquent eyebrow at Hayley, and was holding out his hand.

'Would you like to dance?' he smiled, and Hayley stood up, smiling back at him, moving into his arms with the ease of an old friend amid the mass of rhythmically swaying bodies on the dance floor.

Victoria was stunned. The force of her misery and jealousy was so great she could hardly believe she could feel like this. She felt as if she had plunged into a pool of total dejection and was floundering around it, unable to swim. Julius Korda was a complete stranger, reminded a frantic inner voice of reason. She knew nothing about him, she didn't even think she liked him very much. How could it possibly matter if he preferred to dance with Hayley, rather than dance with her? How could she possibly care so much?

Somehow she managed to shake off the shroud of misery and dance again with Sebastian, sparkling and laughing opposite his lively performance.

But her eyes were drawn frequently to Julius and Hayley, still dancing together, her cheek against his muscular shoulder, her bright red hair a magnificent foil to his sleek ash blond.

She refused Sebastian's friendly invitation to carry on dancing, and subsided by Andrew. She was too choked to laugh at his gentle teasing, and embarrassed that she couldn't hide her misery from him.

'Getting bored, Vicky? Say the word and we could all go home to bed.'

She shook her head determinedly, staring at her tightly laced hands on the table, not trusting herself to speak. She wanted to rush on to the dance floor, push herself between Hayley and Julius, and claim Hayley's place in his arms.

She wanted to discover how it felt to be that close to him, to move slowly against him like that. The urge was so strong she was quite shocked at herself.

After an eternity, Julius and Hayley returned to their table, and Andrew took his wife off to dance.

Victoria faced Julius across the table, willing herself to be aloof and sophisticated.

'Tired?' he asked quietly.

'No, not at all. I'm quite happy to stay until everyone else is ready to go home. I can hardly drag everyone here then drag them back home again just to suit myself!'

'Can't you?'

She looked at him sharply. His face was deadpan, his eyes hidden in shadow.

'What do you mean?'

He shrugged. 'You strike me as very used to getting your own way,' he commented. 'Do you always sulk when you don't?'

She was dumbfounded. What possible reason could he have for insulting her so deliberately?

'Sulk?' she repeated, in a gasp of indignation. Her heart was thudding so loudly she was sure people near by must hear it, and her hands were shaking so much she had to grip them tightly round herself. 'I *never* sulk! And if you're implying I'm spoilt, or over-privileged or something, you can't have the faintest idea what I'm really like—you don't know the first thing about me! I won't deny I was feeling—sad. But I was *not* sulking! Do *you* always gloat when you catch someone making a fool of themselves?'

There was a taut, charged silence, and she felt almost like crying, her emotions were so overheated. Then Julius's teeth flashed very white in the darkness, and he smiled his devastating smile.

'Invariably,' he agreed blandly, and her sense of the

ridiculous saved her, and she burst out laughing.

'Would you care to dance, Victoria?'

She was about to frame a snappy retort, taunt him about his geriatric inability to keep up with her, but there was a sudden stillness inside her, and she said nothing, turning instead to watch Andrew and Hayley on the dance floor. Her sister's tawny head was on her husband's shoulder, cradled close in his arms as they moved slowly to an old Roberta Flack song, 'The First Time Ever I Saw Your Face'. How happy they looked. They still danced like lovers.

'Well? Shall we dance?'

'No, thanks.' Impossible to gauge what it cost to say it, but immediately her ego felt better, a little self-esteem restored. But when Julius moved his head slightly, and the light revealed his expression, for a moment she couldn't breathe. What she thought she saw in his eyes made her heart leap erratically in her chest, and goose-pimples shiver her arms.

Squeezing her eyes briefly shut, she opened them and stared at him disbelievingly. So this was it, she concluded hazily. In spite of some inexplicable need to score points off each other, this was the amazing, earth-shattering 'thing' they spoke of, which interfered with sleep and careers and turned sane people into gibbering idiots. She was suddenly gripped by terror, overwhelmed with panic at the unknown situation she was tumbling headlong into, and which she felt she had little or no control over.

'Oh, dear,' she breathed, unlacing her tightly clenched hands abruptly and standing up. 'Excuse me, I'll get my jacket. I suddenly feel cold.'

She shivered all the way home, desperately tired but sitting rigidly upright beside Julius in the back of the car. She was horrified at the thought of falling asleep on him. After a few miles her eyelids drooped uncontrollably, and she pressed herself against her own side of the car. Her last thought was that if she had to fall asleep, the arm-rest on her door would be an infinitely safer place to do so than Julius Korda's shoulder.

She woke in pitch darkness, and a silence which indicated the middle of the night. Her throat was dry, and she had an excruciating ache in her temples. When she sat up, the pain stabbed through her like someone digging a knife into her skull, and she groaned, holding her head gingerly in her hands, and trying to remember how she had got into her Victorian pin-tucked cotton nighshirt and into bed. She could remember leaving the nightclub; after that it was a total blank. The only part she remembered with gruesome clarity was drinking far too much wine and making a complete fool of herself.

She flicked on the bedside light, wincing in its glare, then steeled herself to bend down and rummage fruitlessly through her handbag for some aspirin. There was nothing; she rarely carried pain-killers, as she wasn't prone to headaches—or any sort of aches, really.

A search of the bathroom cabinet drew another blank, and, pressing her hand to her forehead she tried to recall where Hayley kept her medicines. Of course, the kitchen. In a high cupboard well out of reach for the day William began exploring on his own.

Half-way down the hall, she got quite a shock when she caught a glimpse of herself in the long mirror by the front door. The white cotton nightshirt, a genuine antique she had bought in a market in Naples, looked rumpled and quite definitely slept in, lacking the modern blend of polyester, and above it her face was only a shade less white, her brown eyes enormous and bruised-looking. Her wildly tangled hair looked as if she had flung herself from side to side in bed rather more than usual. She looked like a very limp, bedraggled rag doll, she decided wearily, eyeing the expanse of elongated athletic thigh exposed beneath the hem of the nightshirt. Well, it served her right. She couldn't imagine what had come over her last night, but she certainly deserved this mammoth hangover, and she definitely wouldn't be repeating the mistake.

Quenching her raging thirst, and downing two paracetamol, she recalled with irritation Julius Korda's abstemiousness last night. That somehow made her feel worse than ever. Far from admiring his almost ascetic abstinence, she felt furious with him. In fact she could quite easily lay the entire blame for her present state on his shoulders, she concluded vengefully. Anyone forced to spend an evening in the monk-like presence of that man, watching him sip that wretched Perrier all night with such steely control, would have been driven to excesses simply to deflect the tension he radiated!

Her progress back towards the stairs was impeded by an alarming wave of dizziness, and eventually she was forced to stop and lean against the wall. Maybe the water had somehow reactivated the alcohol, she conjectured miserably, levering herself upright again and tackling the first stair with dogged determination. But before she had dragged herself any further the light was abruptly switched on, and Julius Korda's tall frame was blocking her way.

Victoria stared up at him owlishly, trying to get her brain to work. Rational thought seemed far more difficult than usual, not just because of her hangover, but because the sight of Julius there on the stairs in front of her, powerfully masculine in a knee-length blue silk dressing-gown and very little else, was bringing all her confused reactions of last night flooding back.

'You're the last person I expected to meet on the stairs,' he said, with a hint of amusement. 'You looked as though you'd be out for the count until lunchtime.'

'Did I really? Well, I woke up with a—a slight headache,' she supplied stiffly, finding speech unusually difficult. 'I came down for some tablets and a drink of water. What are you doing?'

'Similar errand—would you happen to know where Hayley keeps indigestion tablets?' His tone was polite, cool, and she gazed up at him, torn between friendly sympathy and a disgraceful temptation to gloat. So he had indigestion, did he? Well, it just served him right. Anyone who radiated the sort of coiled-up repression Julius Korda radiated just had to accept the laws of cause and effect.

'Follow me, I'll show you,' she said graciously, grinning suddenly as she ushered him through to the kitchen. She started to reach up to the high cupboard for the medicine box, then stopped in mid-reach, remembering the shortness of her nightshirt just a fraction too late.

'They're up there, in that box,' she told him, crimson-faced, clumsily backing away as Julius came round the table very close to her and reached into the cupboard.

She reversed into the table and almost fell over, then propped herself against it for support, unable to avert her eyes from the ripple of muscle under Julius's deeply tanned skin.

At such close quarters, and being so scantily dressed, she was physically aware of him in a way that was completely new to her. There was spellbinding strength and symmetry about him. She had never thought of a man in those terms before. She had seen male friends stripped down to swimming-trunks countless times, revealing a lot more body than Julius was now revealing. But somehow this was different. Looking at Julius seemed to be making her knees weak and her heart thud faster, and yet he appeared to be totally unmoved by her mesmerised observation, chewing two of the indigestion tablets in a prosaic, almost preoccupied manner, then finding a glass and drinking some water, seemingly oblivious of her.

She tried to break the spell that seemed to be weaving itself around her, forcing herself deliberately to look for imperfections, anything which she found unattractive, to try to balance her obsession, but for the life of her in this trance-like grip of admiration she couldn't find anything. All his imperfections looked attractive. The way his blond hair stood slightly on end at the front, the way his large, slightly bent nose looked as if it might have been broken at some stage in the past, the lines round his eyes and mouth which suggested that once upon a time he had laughed or smiled a lot, although he didn't seem to any more, the blond stubble outlining the wide hard mouth and roughening his rather broad jawline—they all seemed infinitely desirable features. The admission filled her with even more alarm.

She felt an irrational urge to touch him, trace her fingers over that strong, aloof, self-contained face and drew some warm response from him. The urge was so great that she hurriedly thrust her trembling hands behind her, and sat on them as she leaned against the edge of the table.

Julius replaced the medicine box and turned his curiously light eyes on her, and she wondered with frantic embarrassment if she had conveyed any of her feverish thoughts to him through the silence. She found herself repeating something she hardly ever did, and blushed a fiery, painful red again.

'How is your headache?' he queried, dispassionately.

'Um—absolutely ghastly,' she admitted, with a slight laugh. 'But self-inflicted, so I can't complain!'

'Do you usually drink so much wine?'

'No.' She shook her head and wished she hadn't. 'No, I don't believe I've ever drunk *quite* that much all in one go,' she confessed simply. 'But I do like wine. I suppose I've been drinking more of it since this summer in Europe. I find it relaxing. And at least it doesn't give me indigestion!'

'That surprises me. White wine in particular is extremely acidic,' he said dismissively.

She experienced a stab of childish annoyance, and retorted rashly, 'But Perrier is even more acidic? Or was Hayley's health food responsible for waking you up in the middle of the night?'

'I don't think the cause of my indigestion is any concern of yours,' he replied, his voice ominously quiet. 'And I suggest you get yourself back to bed. You look terrible.'

'Why, thank you!' she exclaimed, in mock flirtation. 'How frightfully chivalrous of you!' She struggled to stand upright, discovering that as her anger rose so, too, did a threatening wave of nausea. She gripped the table again, shutting her eyes in panic as the floor seemed to be executing rocking motions beneath her feet.

'Are you all right, Victoria? You're very pale.'

'Yes, well——' she gasped, trying to make a joke of her dilemma, 'just don't pay me any more compliments tonight, I don't think I can cope with them.'

She was desperately aware that she had to get to the bathroom quickly, and took a step towards the door, cursing the way the floor seemed to slope away from her like the deck of a ship in a storm. Julius hastily slammed down his glass of water, and was beside her in two strides.

'Come on, I'll help you to the bathroom,' he said flatly, taking such instant charge she hardly had time to wallow in acute embarassment. Within five seconds, she was gasping miserably over the basin in the downstairs cloakroom, supported by the hardness of Julius's arm round her shoulders, his fingers holding her head.

She retched until she feared the lining of her stomach might come away, then collapsed weakly against the basin while he ran the tap and rinsed her face efficiently with cold water.

'Oh, dear! How dreadful—I'm so sorry——' she moaned, her face suddenly muffled against his chest as he swung her up into his arms and carried her towards the stairs. In spite of her fragile state, her senses were still powerfully aware of him as he held her close to his body. Shutting her eyes tightly to blot out his visual image didn't help at all, because she could feel shivers of sensation on the back of her thighs where his arm encircled her legs, the slight roughness of his chest hair against her cheek, almost unbearably intimate in the circumstances.

She found herself marvelling in the warmth of his skin. Somehow she had imagined him cold, like his personality, but he wasn't, he was warm and smelled faintly of lemon, a clean, fresh, masculine aroma which stirred her pulses.

Fingers of greyish light were stealing along the landing as they reached her room, and she was dimly aware that the birds were beginning their early morning chorus. Faint bumping, cooing and rattling sounds from William's room indicated that he was already wide awake and playing with the activity centre strapped to his cot.

'Oh, no, that's all I need. Hayley will be up making wholemeal pancakes or something in an hour or so!' she groaned. Julius said nothing as he bent to deposit her on the bed. No doubt he had no words to express his feelings of contempt and disgust, she thought despairingly. If it wasn't so tragic, the situation might be funny. How *not* to impress the man you most wanted to impress!

Her nightshirt rode disastrously high on her thighs as he pulled the duvet out to cover her, and she was relieved when privacy was restored by the warmth of the quilt. She gazed up at his dark shape, his expression unfathomable in the shadowy dawn light, and sleepy gratitude cheered her a little. He might despise her, but at least he had helped.

'Thank you,' she murmured indistinctly, finding even more difficulty getting her tongue round her words. 'That really *was* most chivalrous of you!'

'Go to sleep, Victoria,' he said quietly, tonelessly, as if speaking to a tiresome child, then just before turning away he reached down and felt her forehead, with a cool, impersonal touch, as if he was checking for a fever.

When he had gone, she closed her eyes, and examined the physical and mental imprint of his fingers on her skin, and a delicious warmth began to lap over her, lulling her into the deepest sleep she had ever had.

Hayley's voice woke her; she stirred and yawned in her warm nest of bedclothes and opened her eyes to see her sister perched on the end of her bed, with a steaming mug of coffee.

'Come on, drink this. You'll feel better. I wouldn't have woken you, only I've got to pop William round to Dr Clements. He's got gunge coming out of that ear he had the antibiotics for, so I think it's infected again.'

'Oh, the poor little soul.' Victoria pulled herself cautiously up against the pillows and shielded her eyes from the brilliant sunlight as the curtains were whisked open.

'Another gorgeous September day,' Hayley commented, her expression only marginally sympathetic as Victoria blinked dazedly. 'Dad can get on and finish harvesting, and I've told him you and Julius will go over this morning and finish looking round.'

'Me? Why me?' she asked with a stab of panic. 'Why can't Andrew go with him?'

She sipped her coffee absently and grimaced. It tasted peculiar, bitter and nauseating, and she put it on the bedside table. Her tastebuds felt decimated.

'Why not you? You know all the ins and outs and hidey-holes of the farm better than anyone, and Andy's had to go into the office. Even though it's his weekend off. Apparently half the staff have gone down with the flu,' Hayley said, sounding less than pleased. It was a bone of contention with Hayley that Andrew's firm of estate agents now opened all weekend, and occasionally disrupted her precious family weekends because of it. 'So, it's all up to you, love,' Hayley said briskly, laughing at Victoria's pale countenance.

'All right, only I had this most awful dream. I dreamt I was violently ill in the night and Julius Korda witnessed the whole thing!' she confided, with a sheepish grin.

'You were. He did.'

'What? Oh, no! So I was! So he did! Oh, and he *told* you?' she howled on a rising note of despair. 'I suppose he told you both over breakfast. What a good joke!'

She could just imagine the sadistic amusement he must have derived from the incident, she reflected bitterly.

'No, he just told *me*. He said you'd been unwell in the night and might appreciate a long lie-in,' Hayley told her, thoughtfully. 'You did rather overdo the wine last night. What came over you?'

'I don't know! I'm not sure,' she said ruefully, avoiding Hayley's eyes. 'Was I really dreadful?'

Hayley laughed. 'Of course you weren't. I thought you were incredibly funny. Especially when you wafted us all off to Options, and went into that aerobic routine on the dance floor!' Victoria groaned, and turned her head into the pillow. 'And that friend of yours, Sebastian. He seems awfully nice. He rang this morning, offering you a lift back to Exeter next term.'

Victoria didn't comment, and Hayley persisted.

'Only it's not Sebastian who matters, is it? It's Julius—am I right? It's none of my business, I know. You're old enough to know what you want.'

Hayley sounded pensive, as if she were holding back her own approval or disapproval.

Victoria sat up straight, her face bleak.

'It makes no difference. After what happened last night, Julius Korda isn't ever going to want to come within ten yards of me again. I doubt if it's the peak of romantic fantasies, watching someone vomit into a washbasin.'

Her sister stared at her forlorn face, and burst out laughing.

'Oh, Vicky! You're so funny when you're looking penitent!'

Victoria chewed her lip, then felt a giggle well up uncontrollably. They clutched each other weakly, and the more she laughed the funnier everything seemed until the laughter tipped over the brink into sobs of frustration, and Hayley gently extricated herself. She fetched a box of tissues from the dressing-table.

'Come on. Cheer up. Get up and have a lovely hot bath. You'll feel much better. And I've got to go, I'm due at the surgery in fifteen miutes. See you later.'

Hayley was right, Victoria decided, drying herself vigorously, and fluffing talcum powder everywhere. She pulled on a cool yellow flying-suit, belted it with a soft white leather belt and added matching white trainers. She had washed her hair, towelled it well, and decided to let it dry naturally, and went downstairs in search of breakfast.

Julius was reading the morning papers in the kitchen, a

pair of steel-framed reading-glasses on his nose. He looked cool and relaxed in the white jeans and another checked shirt, open-necked to show the beginnings of the coarse sprinkling of blond hair on his chest. Looking at it reminded her so forcibly of last night's fiasco that she almost groaned out loud.

Julius checked his watch, his expression unreadable, before he said, 'Good morning, Victoria. I hope you slept well eventually.'

Eyeing the clock on the wall over the Aga, she caught the irony in his 'Good morning'. It was two minutes to twelve.

The coffee-pot felt cold, and she went to re-boil the kettle and fill the toaster, not quite sure what to say.

'About last night,' she began, awkwardly.

'Forget it,' said Julius abruptly.

'Believe me, I'd love to!' she said shakily, laughing. 'In fact, I even woke up this morning convincing myself it was all a nasty dream! But it's not the sort of incident that fades from the mind all that quickly!'

'I said forget it. It was nothing,' he repeated flatly, removing the reading-glasses and slipping them into a black case.

'Well, I feel so incredibly embarrassed about it——'

'There's no need.'

The kettle was boiling and switched itself off in the silence, and then her attention was dragged from his level gaze by two pieces of very black toast leaping from the toaster, one of them ending up on the floor.

'Oh, drat it!' she exploded, flinging the offending offerings into the bin, then meeting Julius's eyes with an involuntary laugh.

'Come and sit down. I'll make you some breakfast.' He folded the paper, and pulled out his chair for her. She came slowly across the kitchen towards him and sat down carefully in the chair. It was still warm from his body. She leaned her elbows on the table, and cupped her chin in her hands, watching thoughtfully as he moved around the room with a spare, curiously economic use of energy. She was reminded of the cat-like lope she had watched on their way back from the copse yesterday. He was good to watch. Everything about him, his actions, his mannerisms, gave her pleasure. Except for his detached, steel-grey eyes, reflecting only chilling lack of interest.

'Hayley said you'd like to go back over to the farm this morning,' she said at last, trying to make her voice sound cool and impersonal, to match his eyes. 'I hope you're not going to try to talk Dad into selling you *all* the family heirlooms.'

Julius placed coffee, and toast in the pine rack, in front of her, and dug his hands into the pockets of his jeans.

'I've no plans to talk your father into anything. I'm hardly down here touting for business. I'm doing Andrew a favour. And passing up a lot of lucrative deals elsewhere in the process.'

'Oh, I'm sorry!' Victoria paused in buttering her toast thickly, and ran weary fingers through the damp curls on her forehead. 'I'm afraid I'm feeling a bit mixed up at the moment! This business of selling some of Mum's things—well, I realise Dad needs the cash. He—well, he's not quite so careful with the accounts as Mum used to be. He reckons no self-respecting farmer ever keeps accounts!' She hesitated, anxious to be loyal to her father. 'But I just don't like the thought of selling any of Mum's cherished things. I know it's silly. But the farm and its contents have been in our family for generations. The place is full of history, full of precious personal bits of history. Oh, goodness, never mind, I'm rambling on again!'

'No, you're right to feel sad about things changing. But

which is more important, the farm itself continuing as a viable concern, or the ornaments and furniture inside it? I gather from Andrew the situation could be that serious.'

'You're right, of course. I know you are.'

'But family heirlooms must be very emotive things,' said Julius in a strangely hard voice. She glanced at him, and saw that his eyes too looked shuttered and hard. Families didn't seem to be a favourite subject of his, she decided thoughtfully.

'Well, just as long as Daddy doesn't get a succession of spivvy door-to-door dealers pestering him when you've gone, offering tempting prices for half the contents of the house!' she joked lightly.

Julius's jaw tightened slightly, but he didn't rise to the bait, and she only recognised belatedly that it had been bait. For some reason this morning she felt the need to goad some personal reaction from him, needle him into a show of real feeling. What on earth was the matter with her? Even if he was being his familiar aloof and remote self, he was being perfectly courteous. He had waved away last night's ghastly episode, and he had got her breakfast ready for her. Why was she feeling driven to behave so badly?

She spread a generous helping of honey on her toast, then pulled the newspaper nearer and scanned the headlines while she ate. Julius left the room, and she heard his footsteps on the stairs. She found the print was dancing in front of her eyes, and she gave up trying to concentrate.

'Shall we walk over to the farm?' she suggested brightly, when he joined her in the kitchen a short time later.

'If you'd like to.'

'Yes, I rather think the fresh air will do me good,' she admitted with a grin.

Strolling through the fields at Julius's side, Victoria couldn't help a ridiculous impression of 'rightness', walking next to him. He was tall, over six feet, but her slender five foot eight measured well against him. Her absurd spurt of elation was so strong she had to restrain herself sharply from linking her arm through his, or slipping her fingers into the lean brown hand so close to her own. This urge to hold, touch, get closer, confused and frightened her, but at the same time she felt gloriously lucky just to be in his company.

She wasn't making any sense this morning, even to herself. Maybe it was the effects of last night, she told herself prosaically. Hangovers were supposed to deprive people of rational thought, weren't they? How could she possibly feel this powerful surge of pleasure in the company of a man who so obviously found her tedious and unattractive?

She thrust her hands into the deep pockets of her flying-suit, and kept her gaze deliberately fixed on the misty September sunshine on the lush farmland stretching ahead. She had never really thought of herself as a tactile person before, but this compulsion to touch Julius was beginning to worry her seriously.

There was a coarse, croaking bird-call from some trees on their left, and Julius involuntarily put out his hand, catching her arm. In some surprise she stopped, as he had done. There was the stark, brilliant plumage of a magpie flashing black, white and deep blue through the leaves, and such a flurry of wings and commotion she thought at first the magpie must be attacking a smaller bird. Then she realised the bird under constant harassment from the foolhardy magpie was none other than a huge, majestic sparrowhawk. The magpie seemed intent on driving it from its chosen perch.

'That magpie's crazy,' Julius murmured, in amused

fascination. 'The sparrowhawk could eat him for breakfast if she wanted to.'

The larger, brown-winged bird seemed to be treating the magpie's frenzied attempts to dislodge it with surprising tolerance, flapping languidly away, but always returning to the same branch.

'She knows her natural superiority,' Julius added softly. 'This must be her territory. If she holds her own she knows that feathered thug will give up eventually.'

Victoria glanced at Julius curiously. 'Well, you're quite right, this is her territory. There was a whole family of them last year. We hope they'll nest again near by. Oh, if you'd seen the chicks—and have you ever seen them swoop on their prey? They're amazing to watch . . .'

She tailed off as the magpie suddenly took flight and flashed off into the topmost branches of another tree, and Julius seemed to become aware of his hand gripping her arm, and dropped his hold abruptly, thrusting his hands into her pockets.

'So you're a naturalist as well as an antiques expert,' she said, as they began walking again. 'Funny, I'd have thought you were a city dweller, and wouldn't know a sparrowhawk from a sparrow!'

'Do you always jump to conclusions about people you hardly know?' enquired Julius, his tone evasive.

Victoria pushed her hand through her rapidly drying hair and shot him a look of frustration.

'Well, some people aren't very easy to get to know,' she pointed out fairly. 'So tell me all about yourself. Did you grow up in the country? Or in a town?'

'I grew up in cities. Several of them. My environment was concrete and steel,' he told her, mockingly.

'Oh. And did you have brothers and sisters?'

'No.'

There was growing coldness in his voice, and she knew

he disliked the questioning, but she decided to be deliberately thick-skinned.

'So you're a city dweller, an only child. How do you explain your impressive knowledge of sparrowhawks? Or is your past some dark, holy secret never to be divulged?' She had suddenly remembered Hayley's lack of information about Julius's family.

'I doubt if you'd find our backgrounds worth comparing,' he said coolly, the silver eyes flicking over her with such cutting indifference she flinched. 'You have roots, and close links with past generations of your family——'

'But you must have family, surely.'

Julius stopped walking, turning to fix her with a chilling, intense stare which made her shrink inside.

'My background can't possibly be of any interest to you,' he told her bluntly, 'and frankly, I don't consider it necessary to dish out a full account of it to every customer I do business with.'

Victoria tried not to show how much he had hurt her, aware that for some reason known only to himself Julius was deliberately trying to smash any fragile beginnings of rapport between them. The pettiness of his attitude infuriated her suddenly.

'What's wrong with you?' she burst out angrily. 'What on earth are you frightened of? Do you imagine I've got some ulterior motive for asking about your family, about yourself? Hasn't it occurred to you I might be just trying to make polite conversation?'

Julius dragged his eyes from her furious brown ones, and stared across the fields, a muscle twitching slightly in his jaw. She watched him helplessly, somehow aware that he was repressing his emotions tightly inside him, and full of conflicting reponses, wanting to hit him or to wrap her arms round him and hug him. She balled her trembling hands into fists instead, and tried to slow her breathing down.

Two combine harvesters were methodically carving deep furrows through the golden corn, and Julius nodded to one of them.

'Would that be your father up there?'

'One of them, yes, I think so. Hayley said he was anxious to finish the harvest this weekend. I expect he's giving Tom a hand.'

'Did you bring a key?'

'A key?' Victoria laughed. 'The farmhouse won't be locked. Goodness, what a city dweller you are, aren't you! I suppose the idea of leaving doors wide open all day shocks you!'

'I'm absolutely appalled,' Julius agreed mildly, as they walked on up to the house. 'Particularly if the place is packed with valuable *objets d'art*, as I've been led to expect!'

The tension between them seemed to be relaxing again.

'Don't worry, the farmhands wouldn't know a valuable antique from a disc-harrow!'

'Then we'd be quits,' said Julius, with a rare grin. 'I wouldn't know a disc-harrow if I tripped over one.'

'A disc-harrow,' Victoria informed him knowledgeably, trying not to let her delight at making him smile show too much in her face, 'is a thing that breaks the soil down. Ready for seeds, a bit like a garden rake does. It's attached to the tractor after ploughing.'

'Thank you.' Julius nodded solemnly, and Victoria stepped ahead of him to lead the way into the cool, stone-flagged kitchen, looking round the shambles with a sigh of despair.

'I don't know about valuable antiques,' she said, with a short laugh, eyeing the row of empty whisky bottles lined up behind the flip-top bin in the corner, and the fly-covered stack of dirty dishes on the table. An ancient club armchair by the old stone sink was covered in polythene and newspapers, and Rough, the old Scottie, jumped stiffly down with a rumble of warning deep in his throat.

'I doubt if you'll find anything worth more than a fiver,' she said, squatting down to pat the dog. 'It's OK, Rough, Julius is a—friend?' She glanced up at him with a slightly taunting grin, and then, straightening, looked round with enquiring efficiency.

'Right, where do you want to start? What did you see yesterday when Dad showed you round?'

'He took me on a tour of the house, but so quickly it was difficult to take it all in,' Julius admitted, surveying the scene with a hint of amused distaste. 'I think I'd interrupted his milking routine. I saw plenty of old oak, some of it Charles I, but presumably none of you wants the actual furniture hauled off to auction. I gathered your father was hoping some small, easily removable item might prove worth a fortune. Which is always possible, of course.'

He walked over to the door, leading into the passage up to the front of the house, and hesitated. The doorway was narrow, the passage sloping with age.

'Maybe if I start by checking the paintings and china cabinets.'

'Follow me.' Victoria led the way along the uneven passageway, dark with its sixteenth-century oak panelling, and ushered him into the seldom used drawing-room with a dramatic flourish.

'The silver's in that sideboard. China over there—at least the bits Mother obviously prized are. The rest of it, a few jugs, dishes, and so on, are either in the sideboard there or in the cupboards in the kitchen, I should think.'

She paused, watching Julius swiftly assessing the

contents of the room with obvious expertise.

'Of course, there are hundreds of pictures.' She gestured to the walls, plastered and whitewashed and dimming with age, and the yellowing evidence of pipe smoke. There were pictures everywhere, every shape and size, in sets of four or six, in carved gold frames and plain wooden ones.

'It's the same in every room,' she added, grinning. Julius nodded, his expression businesslike, and she left him to it while she went back to the kitchen to tackle the mess. Mrs Bunting, Father's housekeeper, was no doubt suffering with 'her leg' again, thought Victoria, making a mental note to persuade Dad to replace her with someone more reliable. Since Mum's death, the farmhouse was more and more resembling a pigsty. Unless in his morose determination to be left alone he preferred living in this squalor to having some efficient person fussing around him. That was probably the explanation.

She was lost in thought, sleeves rolled up, with an enormous navy-blue and white spotted apron enveloping her, thinking sadly how spotless the farmhouse had always looked when Mother was alive, when Julius came back into the kitchen. He held a patterned jug.

'Any luck?'

He shrugged, his dark face unreadable. 'There's an interesting Mildred Butler watercolour, which should fetch several thousand.'

Her jaw dropped, and she pulled off the apron impatiently.

'Several thousand? For a watercolour? Which one do you mean?'

'The garden, with the cat on the path. It's in good condition, for 1898; the colours are still unfaded. It hasn't been hung in direct sunlight. And the Irish school is very popular at the moment, with the Americans particularly,' he said concisely, then, seeing her disbelieving expression, added, 'Art is my speciality. I do know what I'm talking about.'

'Oh, yes. Hayley told me you draw or paint yourself. What kind of thing do you do?'

'Not very much, these days,' he said dismissively, holding up the small jug in his hand, shaped like an eighteenth-century coffee-pot but made of china. 'I'm also interested in this—is there any more of it around?'

Victoria went to examine the jug. 'I'm not sure—I seem to remember seeing some more like this, but I can't remember where. It doesn't look terribly special, does it!' She pulled a face at the chipped spout, and another chunk missing from the lid. 'There could be an old vase like this in the chest on the landing. I'll show you.'

She led Julius up the creaking oak stairs to the first-floor landing. The house was a mixture of Tudor, Queen Anne, Regency, and Edwardian, bits being added at intervals by each new generation requiring more space. The floorboards on the landing were uncarpeted, and usually highly polished, but Mrs Bunting's recent absence was in evidence everywhere, however, and a layer of dust dulled the shine.

Kneeling down by the intricately carved wooden chest, her long red curls tumbled over her face, Victoria lifted the lid. The interior revealed a motley assortment of ornaments, vases, some with crumbling bits of green oasis spilling out, and pieces of heavily tarnished brass and copper someone had tired of cleaning. But she had obviously been mistaken about the bird-patterned china.

'Is there anywhere else worth looking?'

Victoria frowned, shaking her head slowly. 'I can't think of anywhere. We could ask Dad, of course. Don't tell me that tatty thing is worth anything?'

'On its own, probably a four-figure sum, I should think,' Julius said casually, ignoring her shocked gasp, turning the jug over in his lean, brown hands. 'It's creamware, made in the Derby area at a place called Cockpit Hill.' He pointed to the flowers and birds on it. 'Hand-painted, about mid 1700s. If your mother had a set, and we could find any more, you could be talking about a considerable sum at auction.'

'I can't believe it. The strangest things seem to be valuable—that nondescript watercolour, now this chipped little jug.' She dimpled up at Julius. 'You know you said yesterday you had no love of the past. But you do love antiques, otherwise you wouldn't do what you do.' She frowned at him, consideringly, then said, 'But antiques aren't the same as people, I suppose, are they? Objects, not people.' She watched how he held the jug, with care and respect, and laughed suddenly. 'Put it down quickly, before you drop it!'

Julius stood it carefully back on a chest of drawers opposite, and met her eyes with a rare glimmer of laughter. Victoria felt the same breathless suspension of motion again, as if Julius's smile somehow drew her into another dimension, where present activities and present time were meaningless, there was only his smile, and her own chaotic jumble of emotions in response to it.

He broke away from her eyes, and looked past into a room beyond. Glancing over her shoulder, she laughed shakily.

'My old bedroom,' she confessed, straightening up, and pushing the door wider open. 'Come and meet Grunt, since you're the expert on antiques.'

An emormous, stern-looking teddy with a very long nose sat in splendour on her pillow, the felt pads coming loose at feet and paws, revealing stuffing, his luxuriant fur now patchy. He wore a red and white spotted tie and nothing else.

Victoria picked him up, and Julius raised an eyebrow in sardonic amusement.

'This has to be Grunt.'

'Yes, it is. Listen.' She tipped him backwards, then forwards again. The bear uttered a gruff, comical sound, a cross between a groan and a growl. Victoria beamed at Julius. 'See? Isn't he adorable?'

'Very impressive,' said Julius absently, taking Grunt from her and turning him over thoughtfully, fingering a large hump at the nape of his neck, and then parting the fur on one ear to reveal a small black stud. 'And also very valuable.'

'Grunt, valuable? Well, I'm surprised—he's falling to pieces!'

Julius shook his head. 'He must be over eighty years old. Turn of the century. Bears like this are collectors' items. Did he belong to your grandparents?'

She nodded. 'My mother's mother,' she agreed. 'But if Grunt is valuable, I don't want to know how much he's worth! And for heaven's sake, don't tell my father either—I couldn't part with him!'

She smiled at Julius as she took the teddy from him, and sat him back on her pillow. 'I've always thought that one day I'll pass him on to my own children.'

She trailed off, and Julius didn't say anything. The silence unfolded between them again. A shaft of sun was aiming its light at them through the open window, and dust motes shimmered in the air. It was suddenly very quiet in and around the old house, a rare lull in the endless clatter of activity on the farm. Apart from the distant, far-off whirring of the combine harvesters, audible across the fields in the clear air, only the slight, settling sounds of the ancient timbers of the house broke the silence. Victoria was aware of Julius, aware of the warmth of his body as he stood close to her by the bed, the slight fan of his breath on her cheek, and aware that the fragile tension of yesterday was returning with a new urgent expectancy. The world around her faded into a void, a world apart from this fierce, fluttering compulsion inside her, and the strong emotion she felt sure was mirrored in Julius's grey eyes.

'Julius—can I——'

'I think we should be——'

They had both begun speaking at once, and stopped again, Victoria laughing slightly, Julius remote and still. With a slight sigh, almost a sob of frustration, she threw her hair back from her forehead and took a determined step closer.

'Will you think I'm quite mad if I confess you have the strangest effect on me?' she whispered huskily. She could hardly believe she had spoken the words. She stared up at his face, catching the merest flicker of emotion in the steel-grey eyes before he seemed to freeze, motionless, in front of her.

'Julius, will you do something for me?' she breathed, almost involuntarily, her voice feather-soft, a mere whisper on an outbreath. 'Will you kiss me?'

She stood her ground, her body rigid with tension, every nerve straining towards him yet almost unaware of it, not even fully aware of the taut frailty of her feelings or her unthinkable vulnerability.

The charged silence seemed to go on for ever. Then with a slight shrug, a faint mocking smile as if he had decided to humour a child, he bent his head and kissed her, very lightly, on the lips.

CHAPTER THREE

VICTORIA closed her eyes. Julius's mouth felt cool and hard, and the kiss was casual, but somehow she was drowning in sensation. Ripples of reaction from the chaste touch of their lips spread through every inch of her body, weakening and melting her and bringing a rush of response so intense it made her feel dizzy.

Julius began to draw away, but she involuntarily reached her hands up and buried her fingers in the clean, silky feel of his hair, moaning softly as she pressed herself instinctively closer to him. Julius's whole body seemed to become tense, and with a muffled exclamation he thrust her away from him slightly, and through dazed, half-closed eyes she saw an expression of such cynical contempt it brought her to her senses with a sharp shock. But before she could retreat, he slid his fingers into her hair, just above her ears, and ran his thumbs down her cheeks to tilt her chin ruthlessly upwards, and still with that sardonic, icy distaste in his eyes he brought her hard against him, arching her body against the steel wall of his chest, then raking a hand down her spine to mould her hips to his own powerful thighs.

Heat flooded through her, and she gave a frantic wriggle to escape, but then his mouth crushed hers, forcing her lips apart and invading the inner recesses of her mouth with shattering urgency.

Her struggles had little effect, in fact they seemed to inflame things even more, and then the pressure subtly altered, from punishment to caress, from rough assault to an intoxicating, mindless pleasure, alluring, consuming her in its heat, promising a world of sensuous exploration just waiting for her to enter.

The new warmth signalled an abrupt end to their contact, and Julius released her brusquely, almost pushing her away from him so that she stumbled, and sat back on the bed, staring up at him furiously, panting as if she had run a race.

She drew a ragged breath, and summoned every ounce of self-control to give a shaky but commendably flippant laugh.

'Well! I suppose that's known as getting what you ask for.'

With a hand that was not quite steady, she touched her sore mouth, and when she looked at her fingers she saw blood. A shudder went through her.

Julius gave an abrupt, horrified exclamation, and dug into his pocket. He produced a clean, dazzlingly white, pressed handkerchief, shaking it open and handing it to her sombrely.

'Victoria—I'm sorry——'

'Oh, please don't apologise,' she said politely, eyeing the tiny crimson spots on the fresh white linen with a kind of interested horror. 'It's I who should apologise. Imagine being so silly as to imagine I've fallen madly in love with a man who finds me physically repulsive!' The moment she had said it, she wished the floor would open and swallow her up. Julius's broad shoulders visibly stiffened.

There was an insistent, irritating stinging in her eyes, and she angrily brushed the back of her hand across her eyes.

'Victoria, please don't cry.'

Julius sounded distant, his voice remote as though he wished himself elsewhere, preferably miles away, she thought miserably.

'I'm not crying,' she retorted fiercely, beginning also to wish herself a hundred miles away.

To her consternation, Julius suddenly seemed to break free of the frozen, rigid stance he had adopted, and he moved to sit beside her on the bed. The hard lines of his face were still unreadable, his expression mask-like, but at least his voice was slightly more gentle when he spoke.

'Victoria, listen to me, please. You must know you're being hysterical. You're certainly not in love with me. And I certainly don't find you physically repulsive. Quite the opposite, in fact.'

She stared down at her hands, gripped together in her lap, thinking that this intensely emotional scene she had precipitated seemed to be taking on unreal, dreamlike overtones. She could scarcely believe she and Julius were sitting in her old bedroom, with Grunt for company, discussing whether or not she was in love with him, and whether he found her desirable or not. Especially since the tone of voice Julius was using was more suited to a boardroom discussion on a business problem.

She decided his determined self-control gave her a perfect escape route, and she took a deep breath, already regretting her painful honesty in blurting out her feelings for him.

'Yes, I'm sorry. You're quite right, I am being hysterical. This must be frightfully embarrassing for you. Shall we go?'

She stood up, and Julius frowned, taking hold of her arm as she would have moved away. Victoria gritted her teeth and met his eyes, finding that he was frowning down at her thoughtfully.

'I don't find this so much embarrassing as—puzzling,' he said, consideringly. 'You're little more than a child, yet your attitude towards me seems——' He stopped, appearing lost for a description. Victoria's cheeks were burning and she felt almost choked with indignation. There was the sensation again of being a specimen being prepared for dissection beneath a magnifying glass.

'Seems what?' she challenged, scornfully. 'Quite grown-up? I am past the age of puberty, you know!'

His eyes flicked down over her high, pointed breasts under the thin yellow cotton of her flying-suit, and he gave a twist of a smile.

'Yes, I do know. But you're only eighteen. Your life is just beginning. You've got another two years at university, and then an opportunity to use what you've learned . . .'

'Yes, I see. And I should try to avoid infatuations with completely unsuitable men. Correct?'

'More or less.' There was a gleam of amusement in his eyes now. 'You're very direct, Victoria. Are you always like this?'

She found she was shivering, perhaps an after-effect of the strong emotions she had experienced in Julius's arms, and pointedly she lifted her arm out of his grip and took a step away from him.

'Like what? Honest? I find it hard to be devious, if that's what you mean,' she said lightly. 'Life's too short to pretend.'

'That's very philosophical. But you talk as if you've hardly any life left to live.'

'Well, I'm not wasting away from consumption or anything, like La Dame aux Camellias,' she countered coolly.

'Then stop wearing your heart on your sleeve,' Julius advised with a cold smile. 'It makes you very vulnerable, Victoria. Sometimes it's not a bad thing to be devious.'

'Spoken by a past master at the art, I suppose,' she snapped, finding she had taken enough ego-battering, and started towards the door. 'Now that I've been well and truly lectured, do you mind if we go?'

'Not at all.' He followed her silently down the stairs and out into the dazzling sunshine.

Bill, her father's foreman, was hosing down the milking-shed floor, and waved to her as she stood uncertainly in the yard. She waved back, realising that she was still clutching Julius's immaculate white handkerchief, now spotted with her blood. She pressed it to her lip again, and checked the white linen—at least her lip had stopped bleeding, she registered, stuffing the handkerchief into her pocket, and walking down towards the gate into the field, her head held high.

Their walk back through the fields was strained and silent, and eventually Julius flicked a sideways glance at her, and said,

'I thought you said you never sulk.'

Somewhere deep inside, a small part of her thawed just a little. She managed to smile back at him warily.

'True, I don't. At least, I try very hard not to. The "offended silence" was one of my mother's front-line weapons. I've always vowed I'd never inherit it.'

'Then will you accept my apology?'

'What for? Cutting my lip with all that repressed animal passion?' she asked, raising her eyes to him in wide, mock innocence. Seeing the darkening of his expression, she looked quickly away, remembering the effect of his kiss on her senses, her pulses beginning to drum. It had been like slow drowning, sucked into a lazily spinning whirlpool. 'No, I won't,' she said at last. 'I mean, I don't want an apology. The kiss was my idea, and if that's the way you usually kiss women, who am I to complain?'

With a stifled sound, Julius's hard fingers gripped her arm again, stopping her in her stride, and twisting her round to face him.

'Victoria, of course that's not the way I usually——'
He halted, raking his hand through his hair, and glaring
at her in obvious frustration.

She swallowed hard, quaking under the laser-intensity
of his eyes,.

'Don't you have any idea at all how—*seductive*—you
are?' he snapped icily.

He made it sound like a shameful fault she ought to
rectify at once, she thought, amused in spite of her inner
turmoil.

She pretended to consider, then shook her head.

'No. I don't think I have, really.' She dropped her eyes
to his hand on her arm. 'Are you trying to stop my
circulation?'

He dropped his hand away hastily, and they both
looked at the red marks growing more defined on her
smooth, pale skin. She rubbed the spot slowly, as he
stared at it in obvious remorse, and then she turned and
walked on.

'Victoria——' He hesitated, and she didn't look round,
keeping her eyes fixed on the path ahead, silently
counting the minutes until she could be back at Hayley's
cottage, and escape to hide her humiliation in the
sanctuary of her own room.

When she finally achieved that goal, she sank on to the
window-seat, feeling strangely numb, and dazedly
seeking explanations for her own behaviour and for
Julius's.

He had been angry with her for showing him how much
she'd wanted him. That much she understood. She felt a
rush of heat all over as she realised he probably viewed
her as some kind of teenage nymphomaniac. The
contempt in his eyes still haunted her, the distaste she had
seen in his face when he'd crushed her against him and
proceeded to kiss her so brutally, presumably to teach her

a lesson. But then, for a brief few moments he had seemed to relent again, and there had been a warmth, a tenderness in their physical contact before he'd pushed her away from him. She shuddered inwardly at the memory of her reactions to that short, blissful union, the tingle of heat inside her, in places she preferred not to analyse too carefully.

Did he see her as a sex-mad Lolita trying to seduce him?

She stood up restlessly, and went into the en-suite bathroom, tiled in peach and white to match her room. Running the cold tap, she splashed her face, rinsing her sore mouth carefully. Julius probably had the impression that she made a habit of throwing herself at any available male, she decided ruefully, seeing the comic side of the situation. The numerous boyfriends who had been hard pressed to obtain more than the occasional maidenly peck on the cheek would be astonished if they had witnessed the steamy little scene at the farm this afternoon. She fervently wished she could account for it, herself. But she was rather bewildered by her abandoned reaction to Julius's touch. Nothing in her previous uncomplicated life seemed to have prepared her for this deep, primeval cauldron of emotions Julius Korda had stirred up inside her.

She plucked a peach-coloured tissue from the box thoughtfully provided by Hayley, and blew her nose, eyeing her reflection in the mirror without enthusiasm. She had always thought of herself as a sensible, well-balanced sort of person. Admittedly her course tutor last term, Professor Fowler, had criticised her occasional lapse into romantic fantasy in her historical essays, but she was generally considered to have a fairly good analytical brain, and was treated by her friends as someone who dished out sound advice and down-to-earth opinions.

Leaning forward, she examined her mouth more closely. It had split slightly on the inside, presumably where the soft flesh of her full lower lip had been ground against her teeth. She touched the swollen spot with her tongue, then, remembering the bloodstained hankerchief, she fished it out of her pocket, rinsed it under the cold tap to loosen the stains, then rubbed white toilet soap over it and swished it around in warm water. Who normally laundered his handkerchiefs so beautifully? she wondered. Maybe he washed them himself. She smiled involuntarily at the thought. It wouldn't surprise her. She had a sudden, clear mental picture of Julius, living in some austere, functional flat in the centre of London, meticulously tidy, like an officer's room in an army barracks, washing and ironing his own shirts and handkerchiefs because no one else could be trusted to achieve the requisite high standard.

She mocked her fantasising. Her guesswork was probably wildly off the mark. He probably had a live-in lover devoted to his every need. Or maybe he sent everything to the laundry!

In a sudden wave of depression she realised it was unlikely she would ever find out. Julius Korda was obviously an intensely private man, who swiftly erected barricades against any kind of intrusion into his personal life. After all, Hayley had known him for years, yet even she admitted she knew little about his past, his family, or his life-style.

Fresh mortification swept over her as she recalled her ingenuous behaviour at the farm, her naïve confession of her feelings for him. She clenched her fists in frustration. Why on earth had she done it? Weren't you supposed to play it terribly cool at such times? Feign sophisticated indifference? Even resort to a spot of teasing flirtatiousness? She groaned aloud as she relived the humiliation of Julius's disapproving lecture. She should have laughed it off—anything, in short, apart from blurting out that she had fallen madly in love with him!

People just didn't fall madly in love in the space of a single weekend. Or at least, if they did they certainly didn't admit it, when the object of their affections was so patently lukewarm about the whole thing.

She glared censoriously at her reflection in the mirror, despairing of the open, childish features. How did you succeed in hiding your feelings with a face that mirrored every thought?

Wide-apart brown eyes, flecked with specks the colour of toffee, gazed back at her unrepentantly, and she compressed the wide, too wide mouth, full-lipped and with its aggravating gap at the centre, where her lips formed a permanent tiny 'O' of surprise. She did look quite ridiculously young. She had an unlined, unlived-in sort of face—no imprint of experience or character on it. A blank page.

In the absence of a mask to hide behind, it was going to be extremely difficult to get through the rest of this weekend in the sardonic presence of Julius Korda, she decided miserably.

Her worst fears were confirmed as soon as she went back downstairs. Andrew had rung to say he would be delayed at the office until around five, although by way of a peace offering he had apparently booked four seats for the Royal Shakespeare Theatre that evening, and Hayley insisted that Julius take Victoria for lunch somewhere, claiming far too much to do in the house to be able to join them.

Victoria was appalled at the prospect of lunching alone with Julius, but she could hardly refuse, and with a sinking heart she climbed into Julius's car, sitting next to him in embarrassed silence as they drove out to a pub a few miles out of the village.

The Golden Lion had recently been transformed from a
very ordinary, tobacco-stained public house popular with
all the local farmworkers for a quick pie and a pint, into a
rather up-market hostelry, with lots of stripped wood and
trailing foliage, and a coveted mention in this year's Egon
Ronay's pub-food guide.

The September sun was still shining, so they chose a
table in the newly tacked-on conservatory, filled with old
pine and jungle greenery, and affording an inspiring view
across her father's undulating farmland, bathed in hazy
autumn mist.

She eyed Julius across the table, tense and
apprehensive, expecting a very uncomfortable meal from
the aloof detachment of his expression. But Julius could
clearly rise to the occasion when absolutely necessary, and
he surprised her by being polite and attentive, skilfully
steering the conversation over a wide variety of neutral
topics which she found herself discussing animatedly.

It wasn't until they had almost finished eating that she
realised the trap she'd fallen into. Her tension had been
translated into nervous chattering. She had expounded
her fondness, with much emphatic gesticulation, for
Beethoven's piano concertos, folk festivals, Italian food,
gymnastics, swimming and disco dancing, and Julius had
paid her the flattering compliment of listening without
actually giving away any of his own preferences.

As the waiter removed their plates she stopped
abruptly, and stared at Julius with guilty annoyance.

'Sorry, I've been talking too much. One of my worst
faults!'

'Not at all,' murmured Julius politely, his eyes
sardonic and amused. 'I find your—vivacity—quite
entertaining!'

This remark struck her as so unbelievably patronising
that she could think of no suitable rejoinder which

wasn't incredibly rude. She kept quiet, twiddling with the stem of her wine-glass, aware of the growing anger inside, positively clamouring for revenge.

She eyed his glass of mineral water, and recalled his choice of something from the vegetarian menu called 'Black-eye beans *au gratin*' in preference to her own meaty lasagne dish. She decided she couldn't resist getting her own back. Draining her red wine, she cupped her chin in her hands and fixed him with a slow, puzzled smile.

'You don't give much away, do you? Are you a worrier, Julius?'

He sat very still, his eyes half closed as he returned her stare of wide-eyed sympathy. With a twist of discomfort she remembered Hayley's comment about men with heavy-lidded eyes, and thought crossly that in Julius's case, at least, that lazy stare certainly had nothing to do with sexual invitation. He had made it fairly clear earlier on that he wouldn't dream of inviting her to bed with him, not even if she was clad in black lace and clenching a red rose between her teeth.

'Possibly—maybe you'd like to be more specific.' There was a warning note in his voice, but she waved her hand airily at his mineral water, undaunted.

'I mean—you worry about what you eat and drink. Is that because of how it might affect your health?'

'To a certain extent, perhaps.'

She giggled. 'Oh, dear! You do sound pompous, you know!'

'Really?' His tone was like ice cracking underfoot.

'I'll bet you swallow handfuls of vitamins every morning, as well, don't you? And go jogging? Or no—wait a minute, let me think—you work out five times a week with weights.'

'I go speed-skiing in the Italian Alps as well,' Julius put in smoothly, with a sudden, tight-lipped smile. 'And your mockery of middle-aged keep-fit fanatics merely betrays your lamentable lack of maturity, Victoria.'

She lowered her lids under the scorching sarcasm in his eyes, and spread her fingers in mock surrender.

'Oh, I'm so sorry, I've offended you,' she apologised, smiling at him sweetly and insincerely. 'Only I find your rigid self-control fascinating. Do you have an ulcer or something?'

'No, I don't have an ulcer.'

The urge to torment some raw response out of him wouldn't go away. She poured herself another glass of wine from the half-carafe on the table, and a demon of mischief goaded her into asking for the rich-sounding chocolate truffle gateau rolled in marzipan and with lashings of double cream, as Julius asked for Stilton and a glass of port.

'Port?' she queried, affecting genuine surprise.

'I do occasionally drink alcohol,' Julius replied blandly, clearly refusing to be drawn any further. 'I merely don't abuse it.'

'Implying that I do abuse it?' she couldn't help asking. Julius smiled infuriatingly.

'Implying that the more criticism you dish out, the more others are entitled to retaliate.'

'I can see you don't like criticism. Am I right?' she said sorrowfully, shaking her head at him. 'You really have a monstrous ego. None of us is perfect, you know. We should all be able to discuss our faults without getting angry, or feeling a need to retaliate.'

She had gone too far. She saw the steely flash in his eyes and began to quake at the anger she was sure she must have provoked, but then he startled her by bursting out laughing.

She stared at him helplessly, all thoughts of teasing and goading gone. His laughter created havoc with her senses. Her pleasure felt so great it was almost like a pain.

'I would hope to take criticism in a rational, constructive light,' he countered, his voice cool despite his laughter, 'provided I thought the person giving it was qualified to do so.'

'Now you're being pompous again,' she flashed back glibly.

'You're incredible,' said Julius shortly. 'Didn't your father ever put you over his knee and give you a good spanking?'

She sat up straight, colour tingeing her cheeks as the waiter placed her gateau before her with a flourish.

'No, he didn't,' she said tautly, taking a mouthful of the rich concoction and wishing she hadn't ordered it. After a few moments, she admitted defeat, and pushed the dish away, flicking a glance of cautious apology at Julius. 'We must be quits by now, surely?'

'Maybe.' There was a touch more warmth in the silver eyes, and she swallowed, staring out of the window at the misty sunshine for a while, with the feeling that some invisible barrier might have been crossed, albeit temporarily. She fiddled with the spoon in her dish, twirling it around in the cream until she remembered her mother's instructions never to play around with your food, and quickly pushed the dish away again. She looked up at Julius to find his eyes on her with an unnerving intensity.

'Seriously—I really am interested in—in, well, what makes people choose the life-styles they choose.' She shrugged, trying out a tentative smile which warmed as it met an answering smile in his eyes. 'It's nothing personal,' she added. 'Just a hobby, really.'

'Really?' Julius's tone was dry, and she had the feeling he was unconvinced.

'Yes, did you mean it—about the speed-skiing? Or

were you just being sarcastic?'

'Yes, I meant it. I also jog, and I work out with weights,' he admitted, with a fleeting smile. 'Mainly to keep my leg muscles in decent shape. Downhill racing puts a heavy load on knee joints and thigh muscles.'

Victoria nodded, remembering Andrew talking about the subject not so long ago. 'Four times the body's weight, isn't that it?' she said, anxious to impress him with her knowledge. Julius looked faintly surprised.

'Yes, something like that. Do you ski?'

'No. But I'd quite like to. I love most physical activities—though the only one I'm really any good at is gymnastics.'

'Hence the hand-walking skills?'

'Yes! Oh, and swimming—my front crawl's not bad! But I'm hopeless at anything to do with a racquet—absolutely no eye for a ball!'

They both laughed.

'I confess I prefer the loner sports,' said Julius thoughtfully. 'But I don't race seriously any longer. Speed-skiing is for the young—I'm considered over the hill at thirty.'

She eyed him seriously, remembering that effortless movement as he had helped her up off the pine needles yesterday down by the river. His muscles must still be in superb condition. She shook her head teasingly.

'Dear me, all these people worried about the march of time. So what are you replacing downhill racing with?'

'Rambling,' said Julius, grinning as her eyes flew open in disbelief. 'With the odd spot of rock-climbing. I get up to Scotland whenever I can. I've always liked fell-walking.'

She remembered the sparrowhawk, nodding slowly. It fitted, somehow. Skiing, climbing, jogging, walking—solitary pastimes, for a strangely solitary man.

She couldn't see him as a team player. Couldn't imagine him as the life and soul of the local squash or tennis club.

'Yes, I see. I'm fond of walking too. It's that lovely feeling of being pitted against the elements, dependent on your own resources.'

'Hopefully including map, compass and survival bag.' Julius cut through her rather romantic description with a sardonic gleam in his eyes.

'Well, yes!' She inspected him frankly across the table, anxious to take advantage of this rare, expansive mood. She somehow doubted it would last very long. 'Tell me about your vegetarianism—I mean, you seem to have this—this in-built gauge of moderation in all things. You select your food carefully, you avoid too much strong liquor—you'd have made a wonderful Wesleyan Methodist or New England Puritan!'

'Would I?' The heavy lids had half closed again, and Julius was leaning back, sipping his port, watchful and wary once more. 'I'll admit I have an occasional aversion to red meat,' he said at last. 'I spent an impressionable age living next to an abattoir. Maybe that would account for it.' There was self-mockery in his expression.

Victoria gazed at him, her obvious disbelief finally prompting him to continue.

'My—abstinence—if you can call it that, is just a habit. It suits my own interests.' The silver eyes were briefly frank. 'I've always had to be a self-starter. If I'd relaxed into excess I'd have failed.'

He stopped abruptly, and the silence hung between them again. Victoria had the impression he was looking back down the years, remembering whatever struggles and fights had led him to the present lofty heights of his profession. Whatever he was thinking, she sensed he wasn't going to share any of it with her.

'So moderation in all things has been the key to your

success,' she suggested softly.

He looked up, grey eyes unreadable. 'Yes, I think you could say that.'

'And by success, presumably you mean financial success,' she hazarded. Julius gave a hard smile.

'What else?'

'Well, I can think of lots of other ways of being successful. What about your artistic talents? Hayley told me you . . .'

Julius cut in on her, the sardonic edge to his voice not completely hiding the underlying bleakness of spirit. 'When you've been passed from one foster-parent to another and end up the most undesirable rebel in a children's home full of undesirable rebels, you soon learn that financial success is the only one to aim for.' The clipped flatness of his voice was somehow accentuated by the cynicism of the words.

Victoria stared at him in surprise. The compassion she felt welling up inside was so great, it took all her reserves of self-control to hide it. But she sensed that pity, even sympathy, was the very last reaction Julius Korda would approve of.

Belatedly she realised she had just been made the recipient of normally highly classified information, and the knowledge gave her a small glow of happiness. She looked away quickly, feeling sure that this, too, would probably not be welcome.

'Well, you're obviously a born cynic,' she commented lightly, aware of an almost tangible relief in Julius's set features as she glossed lightly over his confidences.

'It's a lot safer than being an incurable romantic,' Julius retorted, waving for the bill and holding open the door for her with impeccable courtesy. He seemed to retreat rapidly into aloof formality on the way back to the cottage. Victoria glanced a few times at his remote profile as they drove back down into the village, then relapsed into silence herself. Even if he had succeeded in nothing else in his life, she mused, Julius was highly skilled in the subtle technique of putting people down.

The Royal Shakespeare Company's current production was *The Taming of the Shrew*, and as it was one of Victoria's favourites she sat entranced through the first half, even to the point of forgetting that Julius sat next to her, his long muscular thighs only inches from hers in the darkened theatre. Victoria had prepared for tonight's outing with an obstinate little glow of pleasure, brought about by Julius's reluctant confidences over lunch. Hayley had been quite right—he was a strange, unforthcoming sort of person, but the fact that he had seen fit to give her a sketchy insight into his personal life made her feel ridiculously proud.

She had taken trouble with her appearance tonight, borrowing yet another outfit from Hayley, and in silky black crêpe evening trousers, and a matching white-collared silk sailor top, with broad black and white horizontal stripes, she felt cool and elegant, and happy out of all proportion to the circumstances.

But after the interval, the party in front of them changed places, and a man with an infuriatingly bushy hairstyle completely obscured her view. Julius became aware of her predicament, and indicated that she could change seats with him, and the unavoidable physical contact as she gratefully shuffled across in the restricted space rather diminished her concentration on the last few acts.

Her mind had been wandering away from the intricate beauty of the Elizabethan language and the enduring comedy of the plot in any case, and instead she had been thinking about Julius's surprising admission during the interval that he had never read a single Shakespeare play in his life.

She'd been quite stunned by such a confession. Admittedly English and history were her own favourite subjects, but even so, surely everyone learned one or two Shakespearian plays at school, at the very least?

Pinned close together in the usual mammoth crush in the stalls bar, and unaware of the surprised glaces from Hayley and Andrew, they had talked almost exclusively to each other throughout the interval, while they sipped their pre-ordered drinks. With a certain laconic amusement, Julius had explained how he had spent very little time at school, preferring to play truant and helping on an antiques stall in an East End market. Her obvious shock seemed to afford him considerable sardonic entertainment, but he had laughed quite genuinely when she declared she was spending an evening in the company of a complete philistine.

When Katharina made her final, ringing speech in praise of the loyal and devoted wife, Victoria was mortified to find she had daydreamed her way through most of the last half, her mind full of images of a young, rebellious Julius, in conflict with authority, rejecting his formal education to pursue his own single-minded ambitions.

They drove back to a delicious stir-fry supper, which Hayley had prepared in advance and left all ready to throw into her much-used wok when they got home. Afterwards, the evening was still so warm they sat out on the terrace in the dark, the scent of honeysuckle heavy in the air.

In a desultory fashion they discussed the play. Discussion strayed to Julius's reason for coming down from London, and he described his finds to Andrew, who promised to take a look at the watercolour and the bird-painted jug the next day.

By now Victoria was dreadfully sleepy, a result of her previous disturbed night. She was yawning every two minutes, but she felt reluctant to go to bed and risk missing out on Julius's company.

His secretary had already rung from London just before they left for the theatre, and he had announced his intention to leave very early in the morning. The prospect left her so dejected she was quite alarmed by the intensity of her feelings.

Eventually, when Andrew and Julius appeared locked in a conversation about the antique trade which seemed set to go on indefinitely, she gave Hayley a hand in clearing up the kitchen, conscious of her sister's speculative gaze but not in the mood for one of their usual frank discussions.

'William's a good little soul,' said Victoria, casting around for a subject which would take Hayley's mind off her obvious preoccupation with herself and Julius. 'Sheila said he went straight off to sleep and didn't speak all evening.'

'That probably means he'll wake me up at half-past three wanting a drink,' said Hayley drily, then fixed her with a gaze which made her heart sink. 'You and Julius seem to be getting on very well.' There was an enquiring note in her voice.

'Do we?' Victoria countered brightly, shrugging with what she hoped was convincing nonchalance.

'I've never heard Julius talk about his past before, to anyone,' went on Hayley musingly. 'What's been going on between you two today?'

Victoria was too tired, and her feelings for Julius wee too confusing, too raw, to discuss, even with Hayley. She shook her head, with an apologetic smile, and stifled another yawn.

'I won't deny he has a very strange effect on me,' she admitted sleepily. 'But if you don't mind, I'd rather not talk about it tonight.'

'Vicky, darling——' Hayley hesitated, seeming uncertain, her brown eyes warm on the younger girl. 'I know you're old enough to look after yourself, but maybe I ought to warn you . . .'

'No, don't bother,' said Victoria quickly, feeling colour sweeping up her neck and suffusing her face, infuriated with this new tell-tale habit of blushing. 'I already know. Julius Korda is as cold as steel, ascetic as a monk, and the only god he worships is the almighty dollar. Forget the come-to-bed eyes—totally misleading, I can assure you!'

There was a slight sound from behind her, and she spun round to see Julius, standing in the doorway to the kitchen, his expression remote, mask-like.

'I'm glad to hear you've got my measure at last,' he said, with a twisted, humourless smile. 'I came to say goodnight, Hayley.'

Scarlet-faced, Victoria excused herself, pushing past him and running upstairs to the safety of her bedroom. She leaned against the closed door, trembling all over with embarrassment and anger at her own crass stupidity.

Stripping off her clothes, she ran a deep, scented bath, and climbed dejectedly in. This had certainly been her weekend for saying and doing all the wrong things, she reflected bitterly. Self-defence had prompted those childish, acidic remarks about Julius, and she fiercely cursed her pride. Why couldn't she have been honest, for heaven's sake? Admit she had somehow managed to flounder into the ridiculous, painful throes of calf-love? That at the moment anything Julius said, or did, and every movement he made seemed to have taken on the major importance of a world crisis?

She chewed her lip miserably, trying to decide whether she would have preferred Julius to overhear a confession like that. No, definitely not. She had already been less than discreet on the subject earlier on today. She would rather Julius had overheard nothing at all. She cringed inwardly at the memory of his face, framed in the doorway.

She lay in the bath a long time, swishing the bubbles around with her toes, staring broodily at the pearly peach varnish she had painted on her toenails in honour of tonight's outing.

Voices on the landing outside told her the others were going to bed, and she heard Julius's door close, then sounds of the shower running in the bathroom en suite with his bedroom. Hayley had masterminded this guest-wing, anxious to provide elegant accommodation for her friends from the City whenever they came. The two bedrooms were decorated with a 'his' and 'hers' theme—her own in peach and white, and Julius's next door in more masculine tones of navy and cream.

Climbing out of the bath, she dried herself and fluffed on talcum powder, selecting a fresh nightdress from her drawer, white cotton with pale yellow ribbon threaded through tiny eyelet holes in broderie anglaise around the V-neck, and the full hem. It had a matching négligé, and she tightened the belt securely, pausing only briefly to check on her appearance in the mirror. She didn't want to look too closely at herself, or she might change her mind, falter from the course of action she had quietly decided on.

Picking up her hairbrush, she vigorously brushed her hair until it framed her face and shoulders in a thick, shiny cloud of curls. Then, collecting the white handkerchief she'd carefully ironed earlier on in the day, she crept cautiously out on to the landing and tapped lightly on Julius's door.

Her heart was thudding so fast she almost didn't hear Julius's low instruction to enter. She slipped inside and closed the door, leaning against it weakly as she stared into the room.

Julius was propped up on his elbow, in bed, and he had obviously been reading in the concentrated pool of light from his bedside lamp. An open book lay on the cream and navy striped duvet, face down. A biography of Guy de Rothschild, she saw, *The Whims of Fortune*.

She opened her mouth to speak, but her throat was so dry, nothing came out. Nervously she watched his cynical expression as he flipped off the steel-rimmed glasses he was wearing and placed them on the bedside table. She was mesmerised by the ripple of muscles in the movement. The width of his powerful shoulders and the deeply carved muscles of his chest and abdomen were thrown into exaggerated relief by the light at his side. He obviously didn't go in for pyjamas, she found herself noting, in a detached way. The blue silk dressing-gown he had worn last night was thrown across the bed, but he obviously slept naked.

'Victoria, what do you think you're doing?'

He sounded wearily sarcastic, as if he knew quite well what she was doing but preferred to make her spell it out.

'I—it's not what you think,' she said hurriedly, seeing his eyes moving to the V-neck of her négligé, and down over the smooth portion of lightly tanned leg beneath the hem. Something in his eyes disturbed her. There was an expression she couldn't quite decipher. 'I've brought your handkerchief back.' She held it out, like a white flag in a cease-fire. 'And I also wanted to apologise. Those remarks I made weren't exactly in the best possible taste!'

'Go back to bed, Victoria.' He sounded tense, wary, as if he was anticipating some emotional trauma and was determined to fend it off. 'There's no need to make any apology.'

'Listen—I promise I'm not going to throw myself at you again!' she protested with a shaky laugh. 'But—but if you're leaving very early in the morning, I wanted to—to talk to you before you went . . .'

She trailed off as she watched his stony expression, and went forward on legs suddenly made of rubber, to sit primly on the edge of his bed. She placed the handkerchief on the duvet.

'There. Is it pressed neatly enough?' she asked, with a faint grin. He didn't reply, taking it and putting it on the bedside table. Victoria gazed unseeingly at her knees, locked together in nervous propriety, like a Victorian maiden, she thought derisively.

'You know, it's the strangest thing—despite your being so foul-tempered, and——'

'—cold as steel, and ascetic as a monk?' he supplied flintily, and she flushed slightly.

'Well, yes, if you like. Despite all that, I feel—I feel so drawn to you. I feel as if I want to tell you all my secrets, share all my deepest thoughts. Crazy, isn't it?'

'Insane,' Julius agreed mockingly. 'Victoria, when you've finished your little ego grip, has it occurred to you that I might not actually want to share your deepest thoughts?'

'Well, yes! But——'

'And has it occurred to you that trotting into a man's bedroom at this time of night, begging to share your thoughts and secrets, might just be misunderstood by any red-blooded male worth half his salt?'

The biting sarcasm drew more colour to her cheeks. She began to stand up, feeling it was high time she made a dignified exit, but Julius sat forward abruptly, bemusing her by revealing a breadth of darkly tanned body, with its whorls of blond hair between flat, dark nipples. Catching hold of her shoulders in a punishing grasp, he drew her back on to the bed, a pale fire flickering suddenly in the silver-grey eyes.

'Where are you going?' he grated softly, the hooded eyes containing a new, disturbingly feral gleam. 'We haven't discussed the come-to-bed eyes, yet.'

Slowly shaking her head, she felt a hard lump grow in size at the back of her throat, and the enormity of her stupidity finally hit her like a ton of cold water bursting through a dam. She felt alternately sad, panic-stricken, despairing. She wanted to cry, but she couldn't even do that. She felt as if all her emotions were suspended, frozen, in the laser-cruel gaze pinning her to the bed.

She heard herself whispering, 'No . . . no! I don't—I didn't mean to——' but at the same time her body was betraying her, acting completely independently of her brain. Reading her as easily as an open book, Julius pulled her hard against him, crushing her to his chest and holding her there tightly with a steely forearm, as she listened to the pounding of his heart. After a few numb seconds, with sensations whirling in a jumble through her mind and her body, there was heat, gradually smouldering through the thin material of her nightclothes, growing into a small fire somewhere deep in her stomach. A honeyed warmth she had never felt before was invading her, melting her thighs, and tingling through her breasts. She raised her face wonderingly to Julius's, as the pressure of his arm changed subtly, imperceptibly, and when he bent his head and kissed her gently, lightly, the small fire began to glow brighter, threatening to flicker completely out of control.

'You're incredible, did you know that?'

She stared at him, tawny eyes glowing, and tilting his head back from her he raised a slightly unsteady finger to her mouth.

'Does this hurt?' he asked huskily, touching the slight swelling on her lip. Mutely she shook her head, her lips parting a little under the pressure from his finger, and with a shudder Julius kissed her again, this time in an increasingly devouring, intoxicating, mindless way, his hands moving skilfully over her body, expertly releasing the yellow ribbon at the neck of her nightdress and pushing the thin cotton away to expose her small, tilted breasts to the exploratory touch of his fingers and lips. After the initial gasp of surprise, she was sinking, slipping into a sun-warmed, silky swirl of sensation, with an underlying urgency which grew, expanding and blossoming, until it somehow seemed imperative that her nightdress and négligé were dispensed with, and that she was stretched defencelessly beneath Julius's long, hard body in bed, aware only dimly that for some reason he appeared to be trembling almost as violently as she was.

Her hair tumbled wildly around her shoulders as he gently stroked his fingers over the slender length of her thighs, and she arched herself uninhibitedly closer, twisting and turning as a clamour of nameless need rose inside her.

'Victoria——' It was a deep, strangled moan, as if Julius was making a final, supreme effort at self-control, but Victoria was so lost in sensation that she gave a choked sob of frustration, tightening her hands around his muscular back, luxuriating in this chance to touch, caress, explore, terrified suddenly that he was going to reject her again.

His skin was smooth and firm, and smelt of lemon or musk, a fresh, clean, male smell, and the muscles beneath the surface were a sensual delight, the coarse hairs on his chest, arms and legs an alien, infinitely exciting texture against her own silky softness.

She was conscious of tightly leashed power, of strength held back, and she looked up at him through half-closed eyelids, the invitation in her eyes unequivocal.

'Julius—oh, please! Please don't stop——' she breathed, scarcely audible, against his mouth, moving against him sensuously, fingers splaying across his chest, following their caressing movements with her lips, her mouth open, her mind blank to anything but her stupendous longing.

'Heaven help me, Victoria, I don't think I could stop now if I tried,' he ground out hoarsely against her ear, and moving with a convulsive jerk he pinned her to the bed, levering powerful thighs between her knees.

Victoria felt a split second's fear, a cold terror of the unknown experience she was willingly plunging into, but it was too late for a change of heart, and besides, fear was nothing compared with this growing, frantic, unbearable excitement transforming her into a soft, compliant, trembling body moving enticingly beneath Julius, arching up to him and giving herself up completely to his thrust of possession.

Her hoarse cry of pain was muffled against his mouth, her slight, shocked wriggle to be free of the huge invasion of her privacy lost in the maelstrom of movement and emotion which followed the fusing of their bodies.

Then, a silence, and a stillness, and Julius finally levered himself up from her, his silver eyes stunned and accusing.

'Victoria, for pity's sake,' he groaned huskily. 'If I'd known this was your first time.' He leaned back against the pillow, his face rapidly resuming its unreadable mask.

'I assumed you knew,' she whispered, bemused. 'I thought because I knew, you must know—I thought that was why you were so reluctant.' She was hardly making sense, but her brain felt incapable of coherent thought. She was stunned by the enormity of what had just happened to her.

Rolling on to his side, Julius propped himself on an elbow, eyeing her with perplexed anger.

'I hardly believe what I'm hearing. I assumed from the way you've been acting all weekend that you were reasonably experienced!'

Victoria gnawed her lip, gazing at him in bitter, growing

comprehension.

'Oh, I see. Well, I'm sorry you're so disappointed. I know men are supposed to find virgins deadly boring, but we have to start somewhere, don't we?'

Julius's eyes were scathing. 'Victoria, the point is that girls with some—experience, shall we say—have usually taken sensible precautions. Girls who are virgins very rarely have!'

She closed her eyes miserably. She began to realise that Julius's experience hadn't even begun to match her own. That while for her this had been a unique, deeply tender act of giving, of commitment, for him it had been simply a physical act, probably as mundane as cleaning his teeth.

She considered what he was saying, trying to compute the likelihood of conceiving after just one night with a man. Surely the chances were exceedingly remote? But having said that, she had to confess the possibility hadn't even occurred to her. Mundane and prosaic matters like that hadn't entered her head at all, an admission which filled her with self-derision and clearly baffled a cool, calculating man like Julius Korda.

That prediliction for romantic fantasy Professor Fowler had mentioned seemed to have had the upper hand this weekend. But nothing, no matter how logical or sensible, could have detracted from that urgent fiery need to give herself to Julius, nor the bliss of being here close to him now, still naked in his arms.

But she struggled to sit up, to shake off the magic spell her own fantasies seemed to have weaved around her. Her breasts brushed against him as she moved, and the nipples tautened instantly, bringing all the sensations of the last few minutes flooding back, making her hot with confusion.

'Well, please don't worry,' she heard herself saying primly, 'I'm not trying to trap you or anything! If such old-fashioned behaviour still exists these days!'

'I doubt if any kind of sexual behaviour goes completely out of fashion,' Julius said caustically. She looked at him quickly, filled with a sudden foreboding.

'Are you already married? Is that it?'

Julius's eyes flickered with disbelief. 'No, I'm not already married, as you put it. And I've absolutely no plans to *get* married.'

'Oh, I didn't mean——' She was mortified by his misunderstanding, but he was relentless.

'What's more, that's a very strange question to ask a man *after* you've had sex with him!'

He sounded as if he was trying to be as callous and insensitive as he could in his choice of words, and Victoria swallowed painfully.

'Had sex with? Is that how you describe it?' she asked shakily. 'You make it sound—cheap, unimportant, like having a Chinese takeaway, or something!'

'Which euphemism would you rather we used?' he taunted sardonically. 'Made love? Had intimate relations?'

'Is "making love" a euphemism? I think it describes what I just did quite well,' she said, in a low, choked voice, wanting to cry but fighting against the feebleness of tears.

'Victoria——' Julius's voice, his eyes, had subtly altered, the anger and mockery fading. He seemed uncharacteristically lost for words, and when he spoke she had the feeling it wasn't that he had originally planned to say. 'Did I hurt you?' He was still stroking the back of her arm, gently and rhythmically.

'It doesn't matter.' Her voice was tight, struggling with the lump in her throat.

'I'm sorry. You made it very—difficult for me to be gentle with you.' He stopped abruptly, then with a deep shuddering breath he pulled his arm away from her, as if becoming aware of the sensuous stroking rhythm of his fingers.

'It must be your come-to-bed eyes,' she said flippantly, trying to hide her pain. 'You obviously have no idea of your devastating effect on innocent females!'

'I think you'd better go,' he said brusquely.

She swung herself out of bed, stiffly groping for her nightdress and négligé, which were in a far-flung heap on the floor.

'What happened just now was in the heat of the moment, Victoria,' he went on, his voice terse. 'And under some provocation, that's my only excuse. There's a certain limit to any man's forbearance.'

'Even an ascetic monk's?' she retorted, forcing herself to shape her trembling mouth into a parody of a smile. 'Don't worry—I get the message.'

She was almost at the door, when he said quietly,

'If anything should go wrong—with you . . . you can get in touch with me through my offices in London—De Lember and Greysteils. Or through Andrew.'

His tone was curt, businesslike, the underlying message implicit. Failing the inconvenience of an unwanted pregnancy, he had absolutely no intention of pursuing their brief acquaintance of this weekend any further.

Summoning every last ounce of dignity, she turned and flicked him her most disdainful look.

'Please don't worry. If anything "goes wrong" with me, rest assured, you'd be the very last person I'd want to get in touch with. Goodnight.'

She walked out, closing the door quietly behind her, and managed to regain the haven of her bedroom before the tears began streaming unchecked down her face. She lay in bed, curled up despairingly, as the bitter tears soaked the pillow, stiff and sore in mind and body until sleep came to rescue her.

CHAPTER FOUR

THE April sky was a fresh pale blue, the sun brilliant on a perfect spring day, but an icy wind kept the temperatures well down, and the two red-haired girls waving frantically for a taxi in the cosmopolitan bustle of Oxford Circus caused a lot of heads to turn with their hair streaming out in the wind, their olive complexions glowing in the cold.

They bundled their numerous packages into the back seat of the old-fashioned black Hackney carriage, and sank, breathless and laughing, on to the shiny leather seat, while the driver waited patiently for instructions.

'Well? Where to now? I've gone along with the mystery tour so far,' Victoria said with a humouring smile. Hayley frowned in feigned concentration for a few moments then nodded with a decisive smile and told the driver to take them to the Inn on the Park.

'Afternoon tea, I think,' Hayley explained, as Victoria stared at her sister in amazement. 'It's high time you had a taste of civilisation.'

Victoria groaned, flexing her tired feet.

'Civilisation? Is *that* what you call it? So far, you've dragged me the length of Oxford Street, via Belgravia, Knightsbridge and Mayfair, not to mention the little detour out to that pricey nursery shop we simply had to visit in Pimlico. Why, Hayley? Why me?'

'Because, Vicky darling, ever since you took on that dratted farm you've been in dire danger of turning into a very drab country bumpkin!' Hayley told her, dimpling at her irrepressibly.

I wish you wouldn't keep calling Roundbridge "that dratted farm",' Victoria protested, gazing at the crazy whirl of traffic around them, which seemed to be comprised largely of bright red buses and black taxis. 'Roundbridge happens to be my home, and also my livelihood. A reasonably profitable one, once I can rectify the mess Dad left behind!'

'Well, forgive me for just sometimes wondering if you've bitten off more than you can chew,' said Hayley, in a reasonable tone which defied argument. Victoria leaned back wearily, staring out of the taxi window but not seeing the buses and taxis any more, instead looking back down the traumatic and turbulent events of the past eighteen months.

Admittedly, she had already made the decision to leave university before her father's sudden death, but naturally the idea of taking over the farm had not entered her head. But then after the will was read, leaving the farm between Hayley and herself, she had suddenly seen the light. She'd always known the farm held a special place in her heart, but faced with the suggestion of selling it and dividing the proceeds between them, she knew how important it was for her to hang on to it, to keep that emotive link with her childhood and her family.

It had been very hard convincing everyone that she meant it. And particularly hard financially. There was a considerable sum held in trust for her until she was twenty-one, from the Urquhart side of the family, but, that being still tantalisingly out of reach, she had had to sweet-talk the Bank manager, with the Trust as security, in order to buy Hayley out and keep the nearly bankrupt farm ticking over until she decided on its future.

And that had been the hardest part of all. Her father had, quite literally, drunk himself to death, and during the preceding months had sold off his two-hundred-strong herd of Friesians, mainly, Victoria suspected, because he couldn't be bothered to milk them twice daily. There was profit to be made from the grain crops, but in the meantime the reassuring monthly cheque from the Milk Marketing Board no longer arrived, and, cursed with bad weather and out-of-date machinery, Victoria had found the lean months very lean indeed.

Plus another major problem, which Victoria had only learned the hard way, namely that farmers simply refused to take seriously a very young, very pretty female who was patently in no fit state to carry out hard physical labour. Farming, in the eyes of the neighbouring farmers themselves, was man's work. A woman's place was in the kitchen, in the supporting role of farmer's wife. They were quite open about their prejudices, and feminism and women's lib had clearly made no inroads whatever into their closed, male-dominated world.

She had found it almost impossible to get any workable advice. One suggested sheep, another pigs, others swore by arable farming alone, or were adamant that a mixture between livestock and crops was the only safe course to follow. In the end she'd just had to learn by trial and error. And she still had a long way to go.

'Come on, Victoria! China tea and cucumber sandwiches!' Hayley announced encouragingly, tipping the taxi driver so generously his gnarled face split into an appreciative grin, and shepherding her into the calm oasis of the hotel.

'Relax, Vicky,' Hayley teased, watching the uneasy way Victoria perched on the edge of her chair in the elegant lounge, 'you definitely don't *look* like a country bumpkin now, so there's no need to behave like one!'

Victoria made a rude, very unladylike face at her sister, and sat back, forcing herself to relax, but she definitely didn't feel at home in luxurious surroundings like these. She would rather be in denims, sweatshirt and wellingtons, and be perched up on the tractor with the wind in her hair.

Catching sight of herself in a mirror on the way in, she had thought at first that she was looking at someone else, and she had to confess she felt quite different in her new clothes. This was Hayley's 'Easter treat', and although she had no intention of letting her sister actually foot the bill for all these new clothes, the model-girl hairstyle and the professional make-up, she had allowed Hayley to flash her credit card, unwilling to spoil her fun for the time being.

'I feel like a China Doll,' she laughed, reflecting how thoroughly Hayley had dressed her up. An oyster lace bustiere, with matching high-leg, V-front briefs, frilly suspender belt and sheer, ten-denier cream stockings. Then a pale khaki silk coat-dress, with padded shoulders, discreet brass buttons and long, box-pleated skirt, topped by a cream, pure wool, raglan-sleeved jacket, with a stand-up collar and lots of stylish seaming and deep patch pockets. The finishing touches were high-heeled Alendé court shoes, in cream and coffee leather, and the ostentatiously upswept hairstyle, scraped up from her face and neck, and frothing into a mass of curls just to one side of the crown.

'Can you imagine the consternation I'd cause if I turned up at the pig fair at Stoneleigh next week dressed like this?'

Hayley lowered her bone china tea-cup in alarm.

'Pig fair? Victoria, you're *not* buying any pigs!'

'Well, no, I'm not planning to. But I'm going to go along and see if any particularly plump little porkers change my mind,' Victoria teased, laughing at her sister's expression.

'Over my dead body!' Hayley said vehemently. 'Think of the *smell*! You'd never get rid of it—every stitch of clothing you own would reek of it for evermore!'

'Well, apart from this ridiculous outfit, the only clothes I possess are jeans and sweatshirts. It wouldn't be the end of the world.'

Hayley looked so aghast that she relented, laughing.

'It's all right—I'm really not diversifying into pigs, you can stop looking like that. What time is this appointment of yours this afternoon?'

Hayley glanced at her watch, then scanned the lounge with a faintly expectant air.

'In half an hour. It's only a quick hop over to Harley Street from here—you can either come with me, or wait for me and have some more tea, or something.'

Victoria considered the options. Her feet were so sore from traipsing around in the unfamiliar court shoes, she was inclined to opt for the latter suggestion. Hayley looked more than satisfied with her decision, and resumed her slightly nervous scanning of the room until Victoria frowned at her.

'Is there anything the matter? Were you expecting to meet someone else here?'

'What? No, no, of course not.' Hayley poured more tea, and they chatted about the delightful nursery furniture and soft-furnishings they had seen.

'They have such exquisite things for babies now,' Hayley declared. 'When William was tiny you were lucky to find a cot bumper to match a cot quilt. Now you can co-ordinate an entire room—and weren't the designs absolutely fantastic?'

Victoria agreed. If you were able to afford it, you could certainly surround your baby with anything from clouds and rainbows, to woodland hollows full of pixies and elves, mice and rabbits. They had both had a wonderful time in the nursery shop.

Hayley was talking about William's latest trick of dangling his new baby brother by the heels whenever he found himself unsupervised, but Victoria's attention was suddenly caught and held, strongly, by the distant figure of a man, visible through the doors of the lounge, striding through the entrance foyer to pause for a few moments and confer with one of the staff.

At this distance, it wasn't possible to see his face properly. Running a finger around the high-buttoned neck of her new coat-dress, Victoria allowed small butterflies of alarm and dread to flap, unchecked, in her stomach, and she put her cup back on its saucer with a rather inaccurate clatter.

Hayley followed her eyes, and suddenly sat forward on her chair, her lovely face transformed into a picture of delighted surprise.

'Oh, look—isn't that——? I'm sure that's Julius.' Without risking a glance at Victoria's frozen face, doubtless because she knew exactly how she would be reacting, Victoria thought numbly, she stood up and waved madly.

'Hayley!' Victoria managed to exclaim, her voice low and outraged, but the tall man she had seen in the foyer was already heading their way, and she schooled her features into a blank, polite mask as he approached their table.

Victoria decided later that she now knew why people in severe shock could actually cope with all manner of traumatic experiences with no outward sign of distress. It was rather like switching into emotional overdrive. All you had to do was make the right, polite noises, say the things that were expected, and you could probably confront most crises with a degree of equanimity.

Faintly surprised at her own controlled poise, she found herself gazing up at Julius Korda's broad, achingly familiar frame, and while speech was temporarily impossible she felt her beautifully made-up face arranging itself into a acceptable, if cool, smile of acknowledgement.

'Come and sit down,' Hayley encouraged, obviously determined to keep the social etiquette buoyant to ease the slight tension already pervading the meeting. 'Tell us all about New York!'

Victoria watched calmly as Julius sat down in a chair opposite her, and, summoning her wits, she waved to a waiter and requested more china tea.

'I assume you'd like a cup of tea,' she said, afterwards, with a polite raise of her eyebrows. Julius's eyes revealed nothing of his feelings as he nodded, smiling briefly.

'Yes—tea would be very welcome. Hello, Victoria.'

Startled by the quiet challenge in the last two words, she put her cup back on its saucer with another tell-tale clatter, and kept her eyes level on his face.

'Hello, Julius.'

'Have you finished over in the States now?' Hayley asked, helping herself to one of the dainty little cakes with a slightly guilty expression.

'Yes. In fact I've finished with De Lember and Greysteils, period.'

Hayley gave a knowledgeable nod. 'I heard a rumour—so it's really true then? You've resigned?'

'It's true.'

'Oh, Julius, I am sorry!'

'Don't be.' He accepted a cup of tea, and leaned back in his chair, outwardly relaxed. Only the fine lines around his eyes revealed tension, and these softened as he smiled at Hayley. 'I've no regrets. And I'm not actually on the dole. They're retaining my services on a—consultancy basis.'

'Oh, well done! So now you're free to—indulge your artistic creativity, or whatever!' Hayley enthused.

'Or whatever,' agreed Julius, drily.

He looked very formally dressed for someone apparently bent on artistic creativity, Victoria was thinking, listening to the conversation with a feeling of exclusion. His expensively cut blue-grey pin-stripe suit had an Italian aura, double-breasted and fashionably long in the jacket. The pale grey shirt and blue and lemon striped tie were patently not the chain-store variety.

While he talked to Hayley, Victoria noted with detached interest that his hair was slightly longer, and fell across his forehead a little more. His skin, if possible, looked even

darker, the pale, heavy-lidded eyes just as coldly hypnotic.
Except when he turned on that charming, devastating smile,
as he was doing now for Hayley's benefit. The butterflies
had subsided, leaving a tight, cold knot inside her, a frozen
centre deep within her. Gradually the anger, the panic, the
urge to hurl the elegant china teapot and cups and saucers to
the floor and stalk out of the hotel faded away, and instead
she poured herself a fresh cup with a commendably steady
hand, and listened to Hayley and Julius talking together
with numb detachment.

Hayley was explaining to Julius how she had come up for
a thorough private check-up with her Harley Street
gynaecologist, following the recent birth of her second baby,
and was combining it with a most enjoyable shopping-trip.
Smiling blandly at Victoria, she nodded at her elegant outfit.

'We've been updating Victoria at the same time,' she
laughed, ignoring the mute pleading in her younger sister's
eyes. 'You heard how she took over the farm when Father
died? I honestly don't think I've seen her in a skirt since!'

'Beige silk dresses are not terribly practical in a farmyard,'
Victoria heard herself say, her voice light and unconcerned.

Julius turned to look at her. 'I'm sorry about your father,
Victoria.'

'You hardly knew him.' The retort was out before she had
time to monitor it, crisp, and ungracious. Hayley cleared her
throat, making a great show of checking the time on her
watch.

'Oh, lord, I've got precisely five minutes to hail a taxi
over to Harley Street.' She glanced from Julius to Victoria,
apparently impervious to the tension, and smiled pleadingly,
'You two don't mind if I dash off, do you? It's ages since
you saw each other—you'll probably have loads to discuss.'

'Oh, I don't think so,' said Victoria quickly, feeling the
blood rushing up to pound in her ears as Julius's heavy-
lidded gaze turned thoughtfully in her direction. 'I might

as well come with you, Hayley.'

'There was something I wanted to discuss with you,' Julius interrupted smoothly, standing up with Hayley. 'Perhaps if you've had enough tea, we could drive to my house in Knightsbridge. It's not far away. Hayley could meet us there.'

'I——' Victoria's strangled reply was smothered in Hayley's enthusiastic approval of the suggestion, and with as much civility as she could muster she let the arrangements be agreed on, watching her sister retreating towards the hotel's doors with the growing conviction that this was all part of an unforgivable conspiracy. Hayley must have planned this 'accidental' meeting all along. And the insistence on the elegant clothes and hairstyle were presumably Hayley's rather unsubtle way of ensuring that her younger sister was presented in the best possible light for the occasion.

She was so angry, she could feel her hands starting to tremble, and she thrust them into the deep slash pockets of the new jacket as she followed Julius out to a sleek grey Mercedes in the car park. She wondered what had happened to the black XJS. Presumably sold to make way for a more flamboyant sign of material success, she decided with a stab of cynicism. But the Mercedes was very beautiful. She leaned back on the fragrant leather seat, and allowed just a brief whiff of the seductive world of power and wealth to surround her before cold reality forced her down to earth with a jolt.

She had to keep reminding herself that she was hardly a penniless waif herself. She might be up to her eyes in overdrafts and loan repayments at the moment, but the Urquhart fortune meant she would probably never go hungry.

The silence in the car as they drove through the London traffic was so reminiscent of that first afternoon when Julius had driven her the short distance form the farm to Hayley's cottage in the village that she felt a small, involuntary smile curl her lips. What a lot of water had passed under the proverbial bridge since that fantasy-filled afternoon. And how very differently she felt about this man at her side, with that long, eighteen-month silence between them.

Julius flicked an enigmatic glance at her, and reaching forward he flicked on some music. The muted strains of a harpsichord concerto became softly audible from a cassette through stereo speakers.

'I seem to recall you had an aversion to silences,' he said, his voice mocking. 'Do you like Bach?'

'I also have an aversion to conspiracies!' she snapped, ignoring his facetious question about the music. She did indeed like Bach's harpsichord music very much, but in the present situation that was totally irrelevant.

'Conspiracies?' Julius's lidded gaze was thoughtful as he negotiated the busy Knightsbridge roads.

'Yes, conspiracies! Or are you really expecting me to believe this meeting was accidental?'

Julius raised an eyebrow, his expression unreadable.

'Hayley didn't tell you? I wonder why not.'

Victoria fought a silent battle with her simmering temper, and finally managed to steady her breathing and turn to stare at him levelly.

'You thought I was expecting to meet you this afternoon?'

He shrugged, swinging the Mercedes down a series of side roads, then into a peaceful tree-lined square, halting in front of a tall, white-stucco Regency terrace with black wrought-iron balconies. A large half-barrel of daffodils stood outside one, with an enormous black tom cat squashing half its contents. The cat jumped clear as they climbed out of the car and sat with his back to them, tail swishing disdainfully, on the sunny doorstep.

'That's Sansom,' Julius explained, on a grim note tinged with amusement. 'He hasn't forgiven me for abandoning him for eighteen months—he's having nothing to do with me, and vandalising my daffodils for vengeance!'

Victoria suppressed a smile. Maybe she and Sansom had a lot in common, she thought fleetingly, eyeing the sleepy square with its highly desirable properties with some surprise. Was this Julius's house? She somehow hadn't imagined him living anywhere quite so—established, traditional. The coldly functional modern flat had seemed a far more accurate mental dwelling place.

'It's handy for the museums on wet afternoons,' Julius said with a sardonic twist of a smile, as if reading her mind. 'Shall we go in?'

Following him past a small brass plate inscribed 'Campion House, Julius M. Korda', she assimilated the muted greens, the preponderance of antique pine, with added surprise. The room Julius ushered her into was square, high-ceilinged, ornately corniced, and with a tall, classical Minster fireplace. There was a green, worn-looking leather chesterfield at right angles to the fireplace, and a number of other padded leather wing chairs arranged in a semi-circle, around a low, sturdy-looking pine coffee-table. There was a tall bureau under one window, an intricate-looking system of shelves and cupboards in one alcove housing music centre, television and video, cassettes and records, all in the same mellow old pine. The floor-length curtains were a subtle stripe of olive and stone. One huge oil-painting hung between the two long sash windows. It looked like an original Cézanne, a cold, hard impressionist landscape.

Realising Julius was watching her, she turned to him, the surprise in her eyes obviously readable, because he raised sardonic eyebrows.

'Don't look so amazed. What did you expect, a slum?'

She blinked, feeling her cheeks redden slightly.

'No, of course not.' How could she tell him she had had in mind something much more impersonal, futuristic, the kind of setting where someone who acted like a robot could live in harmony with his surroundings!

A telephone was ringing in another room, and Julius gestured towards the chesterfield.

'Sit down, Victoria. I'll only be a moment.'

He pulled the door to, but didn't quite close it after him, and she could hear his deep, clipped tones, though not clearly enough to make out what he was saying.

The relief at being alone, even only temporarily, was enormous. She found she had almost been holding her breath, and expelled it in a long sigh. But the underlying anger wouldn't go away. How could Hayley have tricked her into meeting Julius like this, knowing how she felt? Worse still, Julius seemed under the impression she had known about it, been happy to go along with it. She clenched her fists in frustration. In the circumstances, it put her in an impossible position, Hayley should have known that.

She didn't sit down, she was much too tense. Instead she turned to inspect the room more closely, and realised that the whole of one wall behind her was lined with books. Unable to resist it, she went to browse along the titles. They were an obscure mixture. A large section was allocated to maps and guides. She pulled a few out, curiously. *Bartholomew's Guide to Bird Watching in the Lake District, Rock Climbing in Scotland*. Ordnance Survey maps of Northumberland, even Dartmoor. She put them back thoughtfully and moved along. Lots of books about skiing, lots of biographies, weighty tomes on the history of art, surprisingly little fiction. A few psychological thrillers. A set of John le Carré.

There was a click behind her, and she turned guiltily, with a ridiculous sensation that she had been prying, but it was only Sansom pushing the door open, entering the room inquisitively and warily approaching her. She smiled, bending down to stroke him. He was lovely, big and solid, with sleepy yellow eyes and an air of rakish independence. He seemed to approve of her, because after a moment or two he lay flat on the floor, and submitted to some under-chin stroking, setting up a fierce-sounding purr.

'You're a beautiful cat, you really are,' she was murmuring softly, then looked up to find Julius standing just inside the doorway, watching her with a strange expression.

She stood up quickly as he came into the room.

'Sorry to be so long, that was a wealthy Arab wanting his art collection valued,' he said, with a cool grin. 'I've invested in an answerphone since I came back. I can't afford to miss out on private connections now.'

He eyed her stiff reluctance to sit down, and frowned.

'Come and sit down, Victoria. Those shoes don't look at all comfortable, even if they do look very sophisticated.' He smiled suddenly, the smile not quite reaching his eyes, and in speechless fury she strode over and sat down with an inelegant bump on one of the padded leather chairs. To make his taunt even more infuriating, the shoes were pinching her toe joints agonisingly; she longed to kick them off, and only pride, plus a reluctance to relax, prevented her from doing so.

'You said there was something you wanted to discuss with me,' she said tightly, keeping her anger well under control. 'Or did you go to such lengths to arrange this meeting just to amuse yourself at my expense again?'

Julius frowned slightly. 'Again? I don't recall ever amusing myself at your expense.'

'Really? Well, it has been a long time, hasn't it. I could hardly expect you to remember such trivial matters after all these months.'

He leaned back on the chesterfield, his heavy-lidded gaze appearing genuinely puzzled.

Victoria felt a pulse racing away in her throat, and wished

she could bite off her tongue. She had absolutely no desire to recap for Julius's benefit that last, humiliating episode between them, his mocking taunts about her virginity, about her ingenuous confusion over the possible difference between 'making love' and 'having sex'.

She looked away, and sought to change the subject, waving her hand to encompass the room. 'This is a nice room,' she said, politely. 'Though I'm surprised you haven't collected more ornaments—*objets d'art*. In your profession you must see the pick of the selection——'

'Normally there are more ornaments,' Julius explained, sounding as if he was humouring her, 'but this house has been let to some acquaintances while I've been away. Anything of value is still in a trunk down in the cellars.'

'Oh. When did you get back from New York?'

'Two weeks ago.'

'Did you have a good time over there?'

'That depends what you mean by a good time,' Julius said, sounding as if he was searching for an honest answer. 'Initially, America is very seductive, very fast and exciting, but my reason for being there was—quite unpleasant. I was investigating fraud, in our New York branch.'

'So why did you resign?' she couldn't help asking, even though she was determined not to show any real interest.

Julius stood up abruptly, and walked over to stare out of the window.

'Personal reasons,' he said, after a long pause. 'Maybe there comes a time, when you realise—enough is enough.'

Victoria waited, curious despite herself, but he didn't expand any further.

'So,' she said briskly, rousing herself once again, 'you got back from the States two weeks ago. And you conspired with my sister to accidentally meet me in London this afternoon. Why?'

He looked suddenly exasperated. 'I didn't conspire with

anyone! I spoke to Hayley and Andrew when I got back. Hayley told me you'd dropped your degree course and taken over Roundbridge Farm. That's when I started to suspect another motive for your actions—they way you used to talk about your chosen subject, your enthusiasm for it——' He stopped again, and rubbed a hand over his forehead, and in the silence which grew between them Victoria could feel every nerve in her body screaming escape. He knew. She was sure now. Before, his attitude had seemed so mocking, but so neutral, giving away nothing, she had been almost convinced Hayley hadn't given her away.

But now she could feel the tension mounting, she could see it in his face. There was a prickling sensation in her scalp, spreading down the length of her spine. It was warm in the room, with the sun coming through the windows, but she had no desire to take off her coat. She felt trapped, threatened, poised for flight. Yet, logically, she had absolutely no cause to feel guilt. This timely reminder fortified her failing nerves slightly. She sat up straighter, prepared for battle.

Julius was gazing at her intently, the silver-grey of his eyes unnervingly penetrating, his anger evident in every line of his body.

'I realise I was a distance away,' he began, his voice suddenly colder, more formal. 'But Andrew had my telephone number. And my office here could have contacted me.'

She kept her eyes fixed on the carpet in front of the fireplace, and Sansom suddenly padded into view, lying down at her feet like a dog waiting to be patted. She didn't move. She couldn't.

'Why didn't you tell me about the baby, Victoria?'

She closed her eyes, and her breath left her in a sharp sigh. It took her a few moments to sort out her feelings, and then she realised that somehow Julius Korda was actually behaving as if *he* was the injured party. She shook her head quickly, trying to clear her brain. This was worse, far worse than she had imagined it could be.

Something suddenly seemed to snap in Julius's tight control, and in a few strides he had crossed the room and gripped her shoulders, pulling her to her feet and forcing her to face him. His ice-flecked eyes were mesmerising and Victoria's throat constricted at his nearness.

'You must have realised I would want to know!' he ground out, giving her a slight shake. 'Have you any idea how I felt coming back to London and finding out I was the father of a ten-month-old baby?'

The heat in the room, his closeness, was stifling her. A wave of dizziness suddenly hit her without warning, and with a frown Julius supported her weight as she swayed and sat down abruptly again.

'Are you all right? You've gone very pale.'

She smiled grimly. 'Don't worry—I'm not about to pass out on you or anything. It's just a bit hot in here.'

'Take your coat off,' Julius suggested with impeccable logic. She allowed him to slide the jacket from her shoulders and sling it over the back of a chair. 'Better?'

There was hardness in his eyes and she shivered involuntarily, gripping her hands together in her lap. After a few seconds Julius turned abruptly and went across the hall to another room. From the opening and closing of cupboards she guessed it was the kitchen. She hadn't noticed that the house was double-fronted when she first came in. She had been too preoccupied with her thoughts. Twisting round, she could see across the hall through the open door. The kitchen looked like some coldly functional hotel kitchen, tiled in white, with an enormous supermarket-style refrigerator with clear glass doors, with salads and fruit visible inside. She could just make out the miniature palm-tree top of a fresh pineapple.

Julius emerged with a glass in his hand, and he gave it to her without smiling.

'Drink it—you look as if you've seen a ghost or something.'

Still feeling numb all over, she took the glass and sipped, then coughed. 'Brandy? In your kitchen?' she managed to taunt faintly. 'For medicinal purposes, of course.'

'Not necessarily,' he said curtly, taking the glass as she handed it back and putting it on the mantelpiece. 'I sometimes cook with it.' She raised her eyebrows, composure trickling back, and he added, 'With prawns and cream, for instance.'

'I'd rather have it with steak,' said Victoria lightly. 'But of course you never touch red meat, do you?'

He leaned his elbow on the mantelpiece, and ran a finger round the neck of his shirt, loosening his tie with a deft tug.

'There are just certain times when I avoid it. Victoria, can we talk about——'

'Is that some sort of superstition?' she interrupted, eyes wide in mock innocence. 'Like never eating pork unless there's an 'R' in the month?'

Julius was silent for a while, eyeing her levelly, some of his anger evaporating. Finally, he explained in an impersonal tone.

'No, it's just an odd quirk of mine. Sometimes, I drink alcohol and I eat steak. Most of the time, I avoid alcohol and I enjoy vegetarian food. There's really no mystery.'

'But you only drink alcohol in moderation, of course!'

'Of course.' There was self-mockery in his voice, and a gleam of laughter in his eyes, and suddenly her heart contracted powerfully and she dropped her eyes. There was something vulnerable about Julius when he lowered his barricades and allowed a glimpse behind the steel defences. She swallowed painfully.

'Well, thanks for the brandy. I'm all right now. It was

just the delayed shock of—of seeing you again, that's all.'
She saw a flicker in his eyes and added quickly, 'And being
dragged around London by Hayley. For someone who had a
baby only twelve weeks ago she's got boundless energy.'

She stopped, watching Julius's expression darkening, and
realising her foolish babble had brought them right back to
the point of conflict. Julius's eyes narrowed.

'Why didn't you tell me, Victoria?'

'Because you didn't need to know.' She stood up to
reduce the towering gap between them and found herself
uncomfortably close to Julius's broad, hard chest. 'Hayley
had no right to tell you.'

'She only confirmed what I'd already half guessed. I told
you, when she said you'd given up your history degree I was
amazed. I couldn't believe you would have done that.'

'Why not? Don't try to pretend you know me—because
you don't, and you never will!'

'Forty-eight hours, a year and a half ago, didn't provide a
lot of scope for getting to know you very well, I'll admit,'
Julius murmured scathingly, the ice-grey eyes glittering
coldly. 'But I must confess, from the brief insight you gave
me, I'd have expected you to contact me when you found
out you were pregnant.'

Heat flooded her face and she glared at him with a sudden
surge of hatred so intense she could easily have grabbed him
by his arrogant brown neck and strangled him.

'Well, that just sums it up, doesn't it!' she snapped,
finding words with great difficulty through her red haze of
fury. 'That's just the sort of cynical arrogance I'd expect
from a man!'

'I told you how you could get in touch with me,' Julius cut
in, his harsh face looking a shade paler under his dusky tan,
the tightening of his mouth revealing his anger. 'And you
knew quite well I'd want to be told. If this was all
some—adolescent revenge because I didn't declare undying

love for you, then you're even more irresponsible than I originally thought.'

Victoria felt her breath leave her in a gasp of shock. She would hardly believe she was hearing Julius speak to her like this. It was almost beyond belief. All these months, since that fateful weekend, waiting, hoping, aching for some word from him, then finally realising she had meant so little to him she wasn't even worth a short note of explanation about his disappearance—the man was a sadist, she decided. A sadist of consummate skill. And he now had the unbelievable arrogance to accuse her of seeking irresponsible revenge.

Conscious of a need to put more space between them, she moved away cautiously until the sofa formed a safety barrier. Then, with a monumental effort to calm her rage, she forced a slightly mocking smile.

'You know, Julius, you surprise me. You seem to assume because you took my virginity—gave me my first experience of "having sex" as you so thoughtfully described it—that you must be the father of my baby! I don't know what Hayley's said, but it needn't necessarily follow, you know——'

'Don't play games, Victoria,' Julius interrupted. She sensed the cold fury he was suppressing, and shivered a little. 'A baby boy weighing seven pounds, six ounces was born to Miss Victoria Francis on June the eighteenth last year, at the Warneford Hospital, Leamington Spa. You don't need a degree in pure maths to reach the correct conclusion.'

She shrugged, holding herself stiffly erect, wishing she were back at home in the safety and tranquillity of the farm. That was where she always preferred to be, at home in the haven of her childhood, with its permanence and continuity. If this meeting was Hayley's idea, she would have difficulty in forgiving her—the last eighteen months had been bad enough without Julius Korda reappearing in her life and hurling accusations at her through clenched teeth.

Somewhere along the line there seemed to be growing confusion over who was the guilty party. She stared at him with a stab of bewilderment. What on earth was he angry about? Had he honestly expected her to do all the running, contact him through his secretary in London and plead for support and assistance during her pregnancy? It defied belief.

'All right. So Charles is your child. But it makes no difference. You didn't want me when we went to bed together that weekend—you made that clear. You made it clear at the time, and you've made it even clearer since. My pregnancy was *my* business—and Charles is *my* baby! So now you've satisfied your curiosity you can push off back to New York, or wherever you like, and leave us in peace!'

'I've no desire to return to New York,' said Julius quietly. There was a muscle working in his wide jaw, revealing his tension. He tugged at his tie again, this time pulling it off in an impatient, fluid motion, and flicking the top button of his shirt open. He looked like a man anxious to be free of constraint, to demonstrate some kind of liberation in outlook. 'I'm no longer tied to De Lember and Greysteils full time. I took the decision to cut loose while I still retained some degree of integrity.' He grimaced slightly, suddenly looking vulnerable for a second. 'I'm intending to paint again. If I can pluck up the courage . . .'

She stared at him coldly. His words made him sound curiously vulnerable too, but she knew better. Julius was as hard as iron.

'That's nice for you,' she said without interest. 'What sort of thing do you paint?'

'Landscapes, so far. Some still life.' He shrugged off his suit jacket, laying it across the back of the armchair nearest him, and running a hand around the back of his neck, as if he was feeling too warm. 'I thought I'd try portraits. They're not something I've enjoyed much in the past, but lately I've felt I might be able to tackle them . . .' He tailed off, uncharacteristically uncertain for a moment.

'Good luck with it, then. Presumably you'll fit this in between valuing rich Arabs' art collections, is that the idea?'

'More or less. And making the acquaintance of my infant son.' The words were calm, but ominously determined. Victoria clenched her fists to stop her fingers from shaking with anger at his arrogance.

'No! If you think you can just turn up after all this time and interfere in my life, because you've discovered you've accidentally fathered a baby, forget it! You must think I've got no feelings at all——' She broke off, breathing hard, aware that her feelings were so mixed up she wasn't sure exactly how she felt.

'I've no wish to interfere in your life,' he said curtly, eyeing her with what appeared to be distaste. 'I wish to make my existence known to our child. I think in the circumstances we should put the child's feelings before our own, don't you? We both knew the possible outcome of what happened between us eighteen months ago.'

'You sound so pompous! For your information, I *am* putting the child's feelings first! What happened between us was a brief, meaningless episode, just one night, Julius! And no child of mine is getting caught in the cross-fire between two people who never cared for each other——'

'I'd think that most unlikely,' Julius cut in softly, menacingly. 'And besides, who says we never cared for each other? I seem to recall some quite passionate declarations of your feelings for me. Are you telling me that was all lies?'

She could feel the colour draining from her face. His cruelty was almost too much to take.

'I was infatuated with you,' she whispered, her voice choking on her fury. 'That means "temporarily deprived of common sense"—I looked it up in the dictionary. My common sense was restored a long time ago. And I can honestly say now that you leave me cold.'

A cynical challenge seemed to flare in his eyes, and before she could react he had moved towards her without warning, with the familiar, cat-like speed, catching hold of her upper arm and pulling her hard against him. The pent-up emotions in his fierce embrace made her catch her breath, and she had to exert all her self-control to wipe out the flood of heat through her body as his sliding fingers warmed her through the softness of the silk, exploring the outlines of the frivolous lacy underwear, the silly suspender-belt and tight-waisted bustiere Hayley had cajoled her into buying and wearing. She froze, hardly breathing, furious with her own physical weakness. She hated him. How could she feel her senses begin to respond to his touch?

With a rough jerk he brought her hips against his, and his unmistakable hardness sent stabs of pure panic shooting through her. She had to dredge up all her heartbreak, all the lonely anxiety of the last eighteen months, to contract her rising desire into a core of lifeless, bloodless numbness inside her.

Julius's stroked the exposed nape of her neck, then tilted her chin up so that he could kiss her lips, his mouth light, restrained, even though she sensed his urgent need to crush her and force her lips apart. Still she didn't move. Could hardly breathe.

He released her abruptly, his breathing not quite steady, his eyes narrowed.

'Well, well,' he murmured. 'You certainly have changed in the past year and a half.'

'Yes. I have.' To her fury her voice cracked, and she turned away to hide her face from his penetrating, all-seeing eyes. 'That should meet with your approval, surely. I always had the feeling you didn't quite approve of my—my adolescent eagerness for sex.' She laughed lightly, masking her turmoil as she turned back to face him. 'You'll be pleased to know that the novelty was extremely short-lived. I've absolutely no wish to repeat the process.'

Julius was frowning at her as if he was trying to understand what she was telling him but couldn't.

'Victoria, what are you trying to say?' he ground out incredulously. 'That I've put you off sex for life?' His cynical mockery was tinged with something else she didn't care to analyse, and the pale eyes raked her disbelievingly.

'Don't flatter yourself it was your cavalier treatment alone,' she countered lightly, already regretting the outburst. 'But just don't waste your time if you were hoping for a quick roll in the hay for old times' sake.'

'You know quite well that's not what I want,' he began icily, but broke off as the noisy rumble of a taxi's diesel engine shattered the peace of the square outside.

Victoria took advantage of the diversion to retrieve her coat from the back of the sofa, and marched into the hall to let her sister in.

Hayley glanced from Victoria's tense face to Julius's beyond, and her expression was anxious and wary.

'Have you talked things over?' she asked cautiously.

'There's very little to talk about,' said Victoria, her fury and indignation evaporating in a wave of weary dejection.

Tears were threatening, and, horrified, she pushed past Hayley into the dazzling sunlight, and half ran towards the waiting taxi.

'Wait!' Julius's voice was peremptory, and he moved with lightning speed to block her way. When she veered to pass him he grasped her arms, holding her still with a casual, effortless strength.

'We have plenty to talk about,' he said evenly, the silver eyes enigmatic as he gazed at her. 'And there's no time like the present, is there, Victoria?'

CHAPTER FIVE

TRAPPED in Julius's iron grip, Victoria gave a brief, furious struggle, then gave up. She was very conscious of the humiliating position she was in, with Hayley watching from the doorway, and the taxi driver observing the scene with undisguised enjoyment. She found the strength to tear her arm out of Julius's hand, and she glared at him mutinously, her chest heaving as her breathing gradually slowed.

Her brain was reeling. Either she made an undignified dash for the taxi, and risked further obstructions from Julius, or she strived for the composure to stay and talk and do all the sophisticated, civilised things people were supposed to do in situations like these. Already she was regretting her earlier emotional outbursts. She raked back some escaping tendrils of hair from her face, and looked around her with a slight shrug, fighing down her temper. She had to see the funny side. It was hard to believe Julius Korda was actually trying to prevent her from leaving his house. That wasn't very sophisticated, was it? That thought comforted her. If she was wildly over-reacting, so was he.

She made a decision, and delving in her bag she paid off the taxi driver, and turned stiffly back to Julius. Hayley was looking guiltier than ever.

'Julius, about tonight. Do you think some other time would be . . .'

Hayley sounded desperately uncomfortable. Victoria at last found her powers of speech returning, and she said with a calm she was far from feeling,

'What about tonight? Or is this another surprise for me?

110

I'm rather tired of being treated like a half-witted child.'

'Come back inside,' said Julius quietly.

'I'll go and make some tea,' Hayley announced determinedly, flinching slightly at the steely hostility she met in her younger sister's fixed brown gaze.

The silence hung heavily in the drawing-room. Julius sat opposite her, watching her speculatively as if he was trying to weigh her up, fingering his chin ruefully as if she had just delivered a hefty punch. Victoria eyed him coldly.

'Well? What about tonight? As far as I'm concerned I'm catching the next train back to Warwickshire. I've got a farm to run and a baby to look after.'

She was secretly marvelling at her composure. The priority in her mind seemed to be to preserve her dignity. With Hayley apparently siding with Julius, and Julius in this relentless, determined mood, there didn't seem much point in throwing a hysterical scene.

Besides, she might still be prone to rash impulses and hot temper, but she had come a long way since their first meeting. She was no longer that naïve, vulnerable adolescent who had flung herself at him eighteen months ago.

She had grown up.

'You have a reliable nanny, Hayley tells me.'

'True. But I also have a lot of important work to catch up with.'

'I'm sure you have.' Julius sounded unaccountably gentler, taking her by surprise. 'But I'm hoping you'll be my guest for dinner tonight. Afterwards I'll drive you back to Warwickshire.'

She steadied her breathing. Every instinct was to say no. But she was beginning to see that the more she protested, the more emotion she showed, the more she would let Julius see her vulnerability. He would see just how deeply he had hurt her by his lack of communication all these long months.

Drawing a deep breath, she asked coolly,

'Where are you proposing to have dinner?'

He relaxed slightly. 'The chairman and directors of De Lember and Greysteils are holding a reception followed by dinner at the showrooms. You and Hayley are invited as my personal guests.'

'Why?'

'It's a preview of a sale starting tomorrow,' he went on, apparently deliberately misunderstanding her. 'The theme is mainly grand bourgeois—eighteenth-century French furniture and sculpture. But there's also something which might be of particular interest to you.'

'To *me*?'

'Well, possibly. Will you come, Victoria?' For a second, she was looking at a Julius she had never seen before, sincere, verging on eager. She blinked. Imagination played odd tricks.

She shrugged, and nodded.

'All right. It appears to be all arranged. I should hate to spoil Hayley's evening, in any case.' She spoke coolly, without smiling, and as if on cue Hayley entered wth a tray of tea, and they all drank and chatted relatively amicably, as if no undercurrents existed at all.

The reception at De Lembers was impressive. One of the rooms had been transformed into a replica of an eighteenth-century French drawing-room, providing a superb setting for a sumptuous array of mantel clocks, marquetry tables, bureaux and commodes. There were so many people there, it was difficult to inspect all the pieces. Everyone who came to speak to Julius appeared to be either an earl, a vicomtesse or an ambassador. Victoria's head began to reel with names and introductions, and for the first time she felt glad of the beige silk dress and elaborate hairstyle Hayley had helped her acquire. The amount of underhand conniving involved in their acquisition still made her boil deep down inside, however. But staying cool was her aim this evening. Losing her temper, showing Julius her feelings, were both strictly forbidden.

Julius was running his hand appreciatively over an exquisite tulip-wood and parquetry commode. 'This should fetch around half a million tomorrow,' he muttered in her ear. She stared at it.

'Imagine paying that much money for something eighteenth-century French aristocrats used to relieve themselves in,' she said irreverently. She had expected Julius to look pained, but he laughed. Her heart did a brief involuntary lurch. It was a long time since she had seen Julius laugh. For a moment she felt disorientated. This all seemed unreal. She had known Julius so briefly, so long ago. He'd been a stranger then, and he remained a stranger now, and yet he had come back into her life as smoothly and arrogantly as an old friend. Just one night, that was all they had in common. But now Charles gave them an undeniable link, bringing them reluctantly together again. She avoided Julius's smiling eyes, afraid of what he might see.

Dinner was laid in another room, leading off the main sale-rooms. The decorations were lavish. A pink and green tented ceiling had been designed, and there were pink candles, pink flowers on all the tables, even pink glazed fruits arranged around the flowers. As the crowd began to filter into the dining-room, Victoria looked around for Julius and Hayley. Julius had been waylaid by a group of glittering socialites some time ago, and Hayley appeared to know enough people to be chatting animatedly about old times in the City. Victoria felt very alone in the crowd, and fervently wished she were back at the farm. When she felt Julius's hand on her arm, she had to hide her sharp flood of relief.

'Well, did you notice it?' he asked, as they sat down.

'Notice what? What was I supposed to be interested in?'

'The creamware, like the bird-jug at the farm. There's a complete set displayed on one of the Louis XV tables. It'll probably fetch more than the table.'

'Oh.' She gazed straight in front of her, and sensed Julius's curiosity at her reaction.

'Did you ever find any more pieces at the farmhouse?'

'No.' She stared at her plate, wrestling with her feelings. She didn't want to remember the past. That chipped bird-jug had mixed connotations for her now, all of them unpleasant. She shook her head, seeking a quick change of subject.

'I thought you said to Hayley that you'd resigned from De Lembers. How come you're here tonight, and in such demand?'

Julius was eyeing her speculatively. She could see he was puzzled by her lack of interest in the creamware. She made her expression as bland and unforthcoming as she could.

'I'm retained as a consultant,' he explained. 'I've still got an office, up at the top of the building. How long I'll keep up the connection, I'm not sure. It's hard to cut loose from everything you've worked for.'

'So why did you?' she asked dispassionately.

'It's a long story. I'll tell you about it another time.'

'Why did you bring me here tonight, Julius?'

'I thought you'd be interested to see a complete set of the creamware,' he said slowly. 'Obviously I was wrong. But I admit I also wanted to introduce you to—well, to my world, for want of a better description. Or what has been my world up till now——'

Her throat tightened, and she struggled to retain her composure.

'Why on earth should I need to be introduced to "your world" as you call it?'

'Don't you think you should know a little more about the father of your son?'

She could feel the fire in her cheeks, and the conversations nearest them seemed to die away into the distance. She sensed their intense awareness of each other was attracting curious looks, and she turned her attention back to her meal, hardly tasting what she ate.

'All you've succeeded in doing is providing your colleagues and customers with some amusing gossip,' she said in a low voice.

'Eat your asparagus,' he advised casually. 'It's steamed to perfection.'

'I find I've little appetite,' she ground back, suddenly longing to escape. She hated the atmosphere here, the overpowering sense of wealth and patronage, of snobbish sophistication and worldly values. If this was Julius Korda's world, he was welcome to it, she thought furiously. What a lot of nonsensical fuss, after all, over a few pieces of varnished wood! The people around her were discussing spending millions of pounds on mere objects. She much preferred people to objects. Maybe that was where she and Julius would always be poles apart.

'Tell me about Roundbridge Farm,' Julius invited, the silver eyes impossible to read. 'What are you doing, exactly?'

'I'm totally reorganising it,' admitted Victoria, welcoming the chance to discuss something she was familiar with. 'I don't know if you remember how it was when Dad was alive. Mainly dairy, with some arable. Well, he sold off the cows before he died. When I took over, the farm was losing money rapidly. We had a terrible year for grain. I sold off over half the acreage to my neighbour, a sheep farmer, in the end. I've recently started a herb farm, and . . .'

'Are you short of money?' Julius interrupted abruptly, and she gave him a militant stare.

'That's none of your business! I'm also experimenting with rare breeds, and some organic methods. So chemical-free vegetables should soon be available in large quantities.'

She stopped, finding Julius's lidded gaze unnerving. She doubted it he was even listening to her. As if he would be interested in talk about farming, surrounded by directors from famous art galleries and professors from the Royal College of Art, and numerous other cognoscenti of the world of antiques and fine art.

With a tense movement she drained her wine glass, and set it down on the damask cloth with an abrupt thud.

'Would you like a refill?'

'No, thanks. I've learned my lesson. I drink only in moderation these days,' she said in a brittle voice. Julius made no comment, but she could feel his eyes on her, thoughtful, speculative, and something seemed to snap inside.

'So you see, I'm a perfectly fit mother. I'm not an alcoholic, I don't take drugs, I'm providing my son with a healthy country upbringing. Are you satisfied?'

'I'm not vetting you, if that's what you're implying,' said Julius with a short laugh. 'Nor was I watching how much you were drinking. You're very touchy, Victoria.'

'Well, I'm very sorry!' she burst out. 'It's just that I'm having trouble adjusting to this extraordinary situation, that's all. Eighteen months ago, you wanted nothing to do with me. Now suddenly you reappear, and require my company at some lavish dinner at De Lembers. If you didn't have an ulterior motive, I'd be completely bewildered! But of course you have. And frankly, I find all this—this mock show of interest, this pretence of caring about what I'm doing on the farm, utterly repulsive. You've discovered you've got a son. Very exciting for you! Why don't you just be honest about it? I'll arrange for you to see him occasionally, I'll even send you photographs of his various "stages of development"—just spare me this insincere attempt to get to know each other better. It's too late, Julius!

Nearly two years too late.'

There was a charged silence. Victoria realised she had probably spoken quite loudly in her anger, and there was a touch more colour in Julius's dark cheeks as he leaned back in his chair, staring grimly into the distance.

'Is it time we were going?' said Hayley, leaning over and glancing astutely from one to the other. Julius nodded wordlessly, standing up and ushering both women out of the crowded room. Pausing only to make their apologies to the chairman and his wife, Julius led the way out of the building to the private car park at the back, every angle of his body reflecting his steely displeasure.

They were half-way back to Warwickshire before anything else was said. Hayley had insisted on sitting in the back, and Victoria perceived it would look too immature and childish if she climbed in the back with her sister. She might not like it, but this situation with Julius Korda was partly of her own making. She had to be prepared to fight it out to the bitter end if necessary.

'Sorry if I embarrassed you in front of your colleagues,' she said at last, in a low, taut voice. She wasn't particularly sorry. She was still too angry to feel remorse. But she was very aware that she had overstepped the mark. Goodness knew what the society columnists would make of it. There had been two or three there, as Julius and Hayley had pointed out earlier.

'Think nothing of it. I just hope it made you feel better,' came the dry retort. Victoria said nothing. It hadn't made her feel better. She couldn't remember ever feeling so wretched in her life, not even when she was waiting and waiting to hear from Julius, eighteen months ago, not even when she found she was pregnant, and finally gave up hoping that Julius was ever going to contact her.

She wasn't sure who she was most angry with, Julius, Hayley or herself. They had both conspired behind her back, and she was going to find it very hard to forgive Hayley for what she had done. But she didn't have to show all that raw emotion. She could have stayed cool, and avoided that emotional outburst. But she had let her heart rule her head yet again.

Hunched miserably in her seat, she stared stiffly out of her window as the Mercedes silently gobbled up the miles back to the farm.

'Can I come in?' Hayley's expression was extremely wary as Victoria opened the front door of the farmhouse.

'Of course,' said Victoria, conscious of strain persisting between them. 'You didn't have to come to the front door like a stranger.'

It was a week since the fiasco of meeting Julius in London, and although she had spoken on the phone to Hayley, this was the first time they had faced each other.

'Well, I wasn't quite sure of my welcome, darling. Am I forgiven for last weekend?'

'I'm not sure,' admitted Victoria frankly, opening the door wider, and eyeing her older sister with candid brown eyes. 'I still haven't the faintest idea why you did it. I've been thinking it over all week, and for the life of me I can't work out why my own sister should deliberately land me in such an unbearable situation.'

For a moment the brown eyes locked, and it was Victoria who lowered her eyes first, and stood aside to let Hayley in.

'I'd love a cup of tea, if you've got time,' said Hayley levelly, flopping into a chair in the kitchen where an enormous dark oak refectory table dominated the centre of the room. 'You're not about to go out herb-picking or anything?'

'No. I'm employing pickers now, in any case. The herb farm is becoming quite successful, in a small way. And I sold twenty angora fleeces at getting on for a hundred pounds each. That's not bad going, is it?'

'No. But it's hardly a living, darling. Have you spoken to the bank manager recently?'

Victoria stiffened. She stared at Hayley suspiciously.

'Is that what it's all about? You're worried I can't support myself and Charles, so you decided to wheel Julius in to bale me out of trouble?' She clenched her hands into fists to stop them trembling, and Hayley sighed gustily.

'Vicky, darling, sit down, please?'

Spinning abruptly on her heel, Victoria plugged the kettle in with unnecessary force, then subsided into a chair on the opposite side of the table. Rough, the old Scottie, climbed out of his basket and came to lie hopefully on his back with his legs in the air, a beseeching look on his shaggy face. She bent to stroke him, glad of the excuse to hide her stormy face.

'Victoria, you've got to stop this! Of course that wasn't the reason I arranged for you to meet Julius again. If you must know, I did it because I know how much you love baby Charles!'

Victoria stared at her uncomprehendingly, raking a weary hand through her mass of red curls.

'I think you'd better explain that statement.'

'I know you want the best for Charles. You want him to be happy. And therefore you wouldn't want to deprive him of the chance to know his father.'

'But why all the subterfuge?' Victoria burst out passionately. 'You made me look a complete fool.'

'If I'd asked you to meet Julius, would you have agreed?' Hayley countered forcefully. 'Of course not! You've become so damned neurotic and defensive about men since you had Charles, there's no getting through to you.'

'I see! And you thought meeting up with Julius Korda again might cure my neurosis?'

'If you must know, I hoped it might. But that wasn't why

I got involved in this.'

The kettle boiled and turned itself off, and Hayley got up to make the tea, bringing the tray to the table with speedy efficiency. The teaset was new, white china with a fresh yellow daisy pattern. Victoria had bought it to brighten up the old black dresser, and made curtains in matching material. She watched as Hayley poured her a cup of tea, and the daisies began to blur in front of her eyes. She took a scalding gulp of tea. She had grown too cynical for tears. She dashed an impatient hand over her eyes, and stared fixedly at the table.

'I got involved because I love you, and I'm very fond of Julius. I'd just like to see you both happy.'

'I see. I wish you hadn't interfered, though. Because if you really had Charles's interests at heart, and mine, you wouldn't have exposed us to the attentions of a man like Julius Korda.'

Hayley's eyes flashed. 'Look, I don't know exactly what happened between you two eighteen months ago—apart from the obvious, of course,' she said drily. 'But I tried to warn you at the time. Julius had a reputation. He'd broken more hearts in the City than I'd eaten take-away pizzas. I could see how you felt about him, but I didn't know how to deal with it. If Mum had been alive, she'd have known.' Hayley smiled briefly. 'She always knew what to do, didn't she? But I was reluctant to behave like a bossy older sister. I was afraid that would drive you straight into his arms, anyway.'

'Whereas I managed to do that all by myself,' Victoria quipped bitterly. 'Just as I can now manage to sort out my life, all by myself.'

'Julius has changed, Vicky.' Hayley said it quietly, watching her for any reaction. Victoria clenched her jaw furiously, thinking of Julius's cold, cynical attitude when he confronted her with his knowledge last weekend. Who did

Hayley think she was fooling?

'It's true. It's not just my opinion—it's common gossip among my old London set. Julius went to New York his old, hard, ambitious self, and something happened over there to change his outlook. The rumour is that the man he exposed for fraud was an old friend of his. Apparently the man tried to kill himself when he was found out. Susan Goodman, Julius's secretary, seems to think they grew up together.'

'Julius grew up in a children's home,' Victoria cut in flatly. 'He told me that much himself. And if you've been in touch with his secretary and his friends in London all this time, I'm surprised you haven't played Cupid before now.'

'Julius rang *me*. When he got back from the States,' said Hayley, emphasising each word clearly as if she were talking to a child. 'That was a couple of weeks ago. You don't imagine I'd have chased after him on your behalf, do you? He rang to talk to me, and to Andrew, and he asked how you were. I had to tell him you'd thrown in your history degree to run Roundbridge Farm. And naturally he wanted to know *why*.'

'So naturally you told him.'

'He *guessed*,' exclaimed Hayley, showing rare annoyance. 'And I saw no reason to hide the truth from him. I *sympathise* with him!'

'Your loyalty is touching!'

'Vicky!' Hayley stood up abruptly, and came to put her arms round her sister's shoulders. 'Listen, darling, please. Maybe I did the wrong thing. When you've just had a baby yourself, you don't always thing rationally. I tend to get terribly over-emotional, I want the whole world to be as happy and serene as I am. Will you forgive me?'

Victoria relaxed slightly, and Hayley hugged her fiercely.

'Julius really cares, Vicky—I know he does.'

'About the baby? Yes, perhaps he does.' She extricated herself from Hayley's embrace, and went across to stare out of the window. Her herd of Angora goats were just visible at the end of the home field. They looked strange and bony without their fleeces. But they were going to be quite lucrative. Next year she would be able to sell some kids for several thousand apiece. She would make the farm pay if it took every ounce of her strength. One day soon her bank manager would welcome her with open arms instead of giving her the slightly pained smile he presently used.

She turned back to Hayley. 'Julius cares about his son. But where does that leave me? Am I supposed to swallow my pride, accept that he never wanted me but now wants what I happen to have produced, by chance, after just one night together?'

'I'm sure it's not like that.'

'Yes, Hayley, it is! He despises me. And even if he did suddenly decide I was the flavour of the month, what I once felt for him is over. I don't want him now. I don't want him, or any other man for that matter.'

'There you go again, lumping the entire male population into one untrustworthy species. If Julius cares sufficiently about Charles to want to get to know him, what kind of mother are you to deny him that right? And to deny Charles that right?'

There was a long silence. The only sounds in the kitchen were Rough's grunts as he settled himself back into the new basket Victoria had bought him to replace the ancient polythene-covered armchair, and the slight tapping of rain on the windows. It had suddenly gone much darker. The big old kitchen seemed full of shadows.

'Let's change the subject,' said Victoria at last, swinging round to face her sister and then darting to the dresser to extract a catalogue from behind a jug full of daffodils. 'Did I show you this?'

Hayley studied it, and looked suitably impressed.

'Very interesting. But surely if Sotheby's are auctioning

the contents of the Mount Cotmayton estate it'll be a little above your price bracket at the moment?'

Victoria leaned over and flipped through the pages, pointing out the lots towards the end of the catalogue.

'No, this is what I'm interested in. Farm equipment. I thought I'd go and spend the night in the Cotswolds and see if I can pick up any bargains. It's a two-day sale.'

There was a knock at the front door, and she left Hayley poring over the catalogue while she went to answer it.

Julius stood there. His expression was mask-like. In tight faded denims, thick-ribbed navy fisherman's jersey and an old green barbour, he looked so very different from his usual sophisticated City image Victoria's insides contracted and shrank inexplicably. The rough, casual attire managed to make him look bigger, burlier, more threatening.

'Can I come in?' His deep voice was impeccably polite, but with an undertone which sent shivers of apprehension down her spine.

She stared at him, tense with conflicting emotions. She wanted to scream at him to go away, leave her alone, to push him backwards and slam the door. Instead she stepped aside and watched as he strolled into the hall, arrogantly confident despite the hostile vibrations he must surely be receiving.

Shrugging off the Barbour, he hung it on a peg and then shook the raindrops from his hair. Then he turned to inspect her, and she became conscious for the first time that day of her scruffy appearance. Ancient rust-coloured cords, flat dusty riding-boots and a much-darned Arran sweater, two sizes too big for her. Her hair, after several soakings in a spate of April showers, that day was even wilder and curlier than normal, tumbling, long and bushy, down her shoulders. Devoid of make-up, she must look absolutely awful.

'Something smells good,' said Julius casually, sniffing the air.

'Oh, lord!' She clapped her hand to her mouth. 'You'd better come in—excuse me——' She turned on her heel and fled down the passage into the kitchen, flinging open the oven door to reveal a quiche, a tray of wholemeal chocolate cupcakes, and a rhubarb crumble, all just turning the wrong shade of golden brown. There was no sign of Hayley, but she could hear voices in the farmyard. Presumably Elspeth was unloading the shopping from her car and Hayley was helping her to bring int the boxes.

And Elspeth had Charles with her. Cursing under her breath, Victoria extracted the hot dishes and baking trays, dumping them unceremoniously on a worktop and turning to find Julius half sitting on the end of the refectory table, looking faintly amused at the scene before him.

'Why have you come?' she asked, in a cool voice, but she already knew the answer. Julius had come to see his son. Before either could say anything more Hayley shouldered her way in with boxes of groceries, and the next few minutes were involved with her delighted greeting of Julius.

And then a sudden silence descended on them all as Elspeth walked into the room, hand in hand with baby Charles. It seemed to Victoria as though they were all staring from Julius to Charles, stunned by the extraordinary likeness between the tall blond man and the tiny child.

But Victoria found herself mesmerised by the expression on Julius's face. She no longer saw Elspeth's fascination, Hayley's apprehension, or Charles's innocent curiosity. All she registered, with a stab of pain in her heart, was the blaze of pride and possessiveness in Julius's eyes as he looked down at his infant son.

CHAPTER SIX

VICTORIA cleared her throat.

'Elspeth, this is Julius Korda. He's an old——' She hesitated a moment. 'An old friend of Hayley's,' she finished up lamely, aware of how idiotic she sounded and trying to avoid Julius's sardonic glance.

Elspeth, brown-haired and freckle-faced, was just a year younger than Victoria, and she was gazing at Julius with open admiration, her bright blue eyes assimilating his features and unusual colouring with obvious fascination. She appeared to be on the verge of remarking on the extraordinary likeness to Charles, then picked up the tension in the air and refrained. With a wave of relief, Victoria stumbled on with the introduction.

'Julius, this is Elspeth Mackenzie, one of Andrew's cousins from Scotland. She helps me with Charles and . . . with lots of other things as well.' She smiled at the other girl as she spoke and Julius held out a lean strong brown hand and shook Elspeth's, bringing a pink hue to her cheeks.

'Are you a qualified nanny?' he asked lightly, and Victoria stiffened. She knew the deeper reason for the casual question and felt furious at the subtle interference.

'Yes, I did two years at college when I left school, and got my NNEB certificate,' Elspeth was telling him, pleased at his interest. 'But I'm getting a bit of experience working for Victoria. That's what all employers want nowadays, isn't it? Catch Twenty-two—no experience, no job, but no job, no experience!'

'Don't say things like that,' put in Victoria quickly,

turning to close the back door where rain was blowing in. 'You sound as if you're planning to leave me, and you know I couldn't possibly manage without you.'

'No, no! I'm here for a while yet.' Elspeth laughed good-naturedly.

Hayley announced she had to leave, to relieve her long-suffering nanny Sheila of William's antics and give baby Jonathan his evening feed, and before she left she gave Victoria a long, meaningful look.

Elspeth seemed aware of the tension, and mumbled something about doing some ironing upstairs. In the sapce of a few minutes Victoria found herself alone in the kitchen with Julius and Charles. She found she had to restrain the urge to snatch Charles into her arms and run out of the room.

'Shall we go into the breakfast room? Charles has his toys in there.'

Julius followed her into a comfortable, slightly shabby room, where building-bricks, stacking-toys and teddies were piled into William's old playpen. They watched as Charles tottered over to the playpen, climbed on to a handy chair and levered himself into the wooden enclosure. Julius shook his head, looking dazed.

'How long has he been walking? I imagined a tiny baby in a pram, not a little boy who can walk and climb!'

'He crawled at five months, walked round the furniture at eight months, and this playpen was never any use. He hates being penned in. It's a useful toy container, that's all.'

'He's only ten months old?'

Victoria nodded, slightly amused in spite of herself at Julius's surprise. 'Elspeth complains she needs closed-circuit television cameras to keep track of him now.'

Charles was climbing out of the playpen now, having hurled a teddy and some bricks out first. Victoria stared at her son, at the lint-white fluff of baby hair, the large

grey eyes, the olive skin and the stubborn chin, seeing him as
if for the first time. He was so like Julius, and yet she had
deliberately forgotten that until now. Seeing them together
was a shock, emotionally.

'I'll just get something from the car,' Julius said at last, as
if gathering his wits. He returned moments later with a
square parcel, covered in blue and white teddy bear paper
and tied with an enormous blue ribbon. He put it in the
middle of the floor, and settled down in a large, chintz-
covered armchair to wait.

Victoria was reluctantly impressed. Most people
overwhelmed small children with jovial attention,
succeeding only in terrifying them. Maybe growing up in a
childrens' home had taught Julius this cool, laid-back
approach.

The parcel revealed a large box with a picture of a sturdy
wooden playhouse complete with chunky wooden people
who lived in it, but Charles was far more interested in the
paper he had just ripped off, and crawled around delightedly
crumpling and crunching it.

Victoria smiled in faint apology.

'I'm afraid he's obsessed with paper. You needn't have
bothered with the present!'

Julius said nothing, watching the baby's antics as if dazed.
There was an unfamiliar light shining in his eyes, and she
found herself longing for him to look at her, just once, in the
way he was looking at his baby son. Then she pulled herself
up sharply, aghast. What was the matter with her?
Memories of her silly infatuation all that time ago flooded
back, and she cringed with embarrassment.

'Would you like some coffee or anything?' she asked, to
break the charged silence.

'Thank you. Black, no sugar, please,' Julius answered
absently. She left them together, relieved to get away. When
she returned Julius was squatting on his haunches, demon-

strating his enviable leg muscles again, and Charles was crawling over him, chuckling with pleasure. The wooden playhouse and people had been unpacked, and Charles clutched one chunky doll in his hand.

The sight of them together, so strikingly alike, laughing, was almost more than she could stand. Her voice sounded oddly choked when she spoke.

'It's nearly time for Charles's bath and tea,' she declared flatly, watching Julius's grey eyes harden as he looked up at her. He rose to his feet in that same effortless movement she remembered so well, swinging little Charles high above him until he laughed gleefully. Victoria suddenly found herself fighting images of those powerfully muscled thighs, deeply tanned, and with their coarse covering of blond hairs. She wrenched her eyes away, appalled at herself, and stared down at the floor.

'I have the feeling I'm being dismissed,' said Julius sardonically, accepting his coffee from the tray and drinking it down almost in one gulp. 'Will you have a meal with me tonight? I'm staying at the Golden Lion.'

She shook her head. 'Sorry, it's Elspeth's night off.' It wasn't, but she could easily arrange for it to be.

'Then maybe I could call back later. We have things to discuss, Victoria.'

She suppressed a slight feeling of panic. There was something relentless about Julius. Half of her wanted to dig in her heels, refuse point-blank. The other half was recalling Hayley's lecture. Her sister was right, Julius did have some claims on his son. She had to be reasonable and civilised about all this.

'All right,' she shrugged. 'I'll make supper if you like.'

'How could I refuse such a gracious invitation?' Julius said softly, a glimmer of amusement in his eyes. 'I'll shower and change at the hotel, and be back by eight o'clock.'

'No hurry,' she said stiffly. 'I'll see you later.'

*   *   *

Victoria was flinging open cupboards in the kitchen an hour or so later, feverishly seeking inspiration for supper, when there was a knock at the front door. She checked her watch. It was only just after half-past seven. Surely Julius wasn't back already?

She glanced down at her clothes, wondering if she had overdone the 'covered-up' look. After getting Charles to bed, and seeing the surprised Elspeth off for a night at Hayley and Andrew's, she had dug around in her wardrobe and found a gathered woollen skirt in a soft wave of rust, coffee and black, reaching almost to the ankle. This she had teamed with a high-necked coffee silk blouse, black tights and low-heeled black patent shoes. One of her mother's cameo brooches finished off the rather prim, Victorian effect, pinned at the throat, and a tight French pleat effectively flattened her usual wild mass of red curls. She had left her face washed clean of make-up, determined to avoid any impression that she was dressing up to appear attractive to Julius Korda. Memories of the past were too painful for that.

Julius stood on the doorstep, casually elegant in silver-beige cords and a matching suede jacket. She glared at him in dismay.

'You're early!' she said accusingly.

'Only by twenty minutes,' he countered reasonably. 'I found it didn't take as long as I expected to shower and change.'

'Oh, well, you'd better come in,' she said, moistening her lips nervously. Catching a glimpse of herself in the hall mirror, she groaned inwardly. She looked pale and tense, like some Victorian governess. Julius was gazing at her with his usual unfathomable expression, but as usual she had the sensation that he could read her mind and was solemnly mocking her.

'I was just wondering what to cook for you,' she

confessed, as he followed her into the kitchen. 'My mind seems to have gone rather blank this evening.'

'Why don't I cook for you?' She glanced at him sharply, but his face was composed, not mocking.

'Are you serious?'

'Of course.' He took off his suede jacket and hung it on a hook at the back of the door, then glanced round the kitchen with a businesslike expression. 'Where's your store-cupboard?'

She turned, pointing to the larder door. 'Beans on toast?' she asked acidly.

Julius raised an eyebrow, scanning the rows of cans and packets and selecting an armful including tuna, rice, chicken soup, mayonnaise. Victoria subsided into a chair by the Aga, and watched his spare, economic movements. There was no denying Julius was good to look at, she admitted, watching him opening cans with absorbed concentration.

'I need a saucepan and a *gratin* dish,' he said, glancing up and finding her eyes on him.

'Fine. If you're trying to impress me with your efficiency, you're succeeding,' she said coolly, supplying the required equipment. 'Do you cook for yourself all the time?'

'No. I have a housekeeper who comes in every day and prepares things. Cooking is something I do for pleasure. I find it relaxing.'

'I don't mind cooking, but it's a lot more relaxing watching someone else doing it!' She frowned, watching him stirring soup, mayonnaise, cream and curry powder in the saucepan, and jumped up to find a large plastic apron, butcher-striped in navy and white, in the table drawer. 'Here, wear this. If you're anything like me you'll be covered in splashes when you've finished.'

Julius slipped the loop over his head, ruffling his blond hair slightly at the front, then fiddled with the ties behind him, with a crooked grin as the tapes stubbornly refused to tie.

'Here, let me do it,' Victoria suggested, tying it firmly round his waist as he carried on with his sauce-making. Standing so close to him brought a strange feeling to her legs, and she backed away hurriedly and regained the sanctuary of her chair by the Aga. She felt confused by her jumbled feelings. Eighteen months ago this would have been the very zenith of her longings, a whole evening in Julius Korda's company. The fact that he was willingly cooking supper for her added a new dimension of intimacy she would never have dared dream of. She had to keep reminding herself that Julius was here tonight, being charming and helpful, not because he found her irresistible, but because he needed her friendship to gain access to his son. A perfectly logcial strategy on his part. She really couldn't blame him for it. It was just so painful to the ego, so bitterly ironic.

Julius was putting cooked rice in the dish, then a layer of tuna, and pouring the creamy-looking sauce over the top having squeezed some lemon juice into it beforehand. He sprinkled grated cheese on it, and sliced a tomato with the skill of an expert chef to arrange down the centre. It looked beautiful.

'Brilliant,' Victoria told him, quite overwhelmed by his cool expertise. 'Now what do you do with it?'

'It goes in the hottest part of your Aga for half an hour and we have a drink while we wait,' Julius explained gravely. The both eyed the scene of chaos on the table, and Victoria found herself smiling involuntarily, in spite of her tension.

'Amendment. The kitchen skivvy cleans up all this lot first!'

Julius shook his head, grinning at her so disarmingly she felt her stomach melting. 'Certainly not. I'm a meticulously tidy cook—just watch.'

The clean-up operation was complete in record time, with such dazzling efficiency she was lost in admiration.

'Your housekeeper can't find a lot to do!'

'Oh, she does. I confess I'm paranoid about tidiness.'

'It's a good job you don't live here, then,' said Victoria, speaking without thinking. Then she blushed scarlet as Julius's cool silver eyes turned thoughtfully on her.

'Is it? I admit I'm also quite paranoid about children growing up with two parents.'

The blush grew hotter, and Victoria put an iron clamp on her wayward emotions. 'In an ideal world, I quite agree,' she said flatly. 'But I'm afraid acting was never my strong point.'

'I'm sorry?' Julius's voice sounded scrupulously polite, but cooler.

'I mean some people might be able to play-act a relationship for the sake of a child. But not me.'

'I see.' Julius appeared to have withdrawn again, his tone reminiscent of the ice-cool manner she remembered only too well. He glanced around the kitchen, raising an eyebrow. 'Do you have any wine we could drink with our supper?'

'Wine? Oh, yes. I think there's some white Bordeaux—I seem to recall you quite liked it at Hayley's that weekend? Or would you prefer Perrier?' She had turned her back, hiding her face from him while she inspected the wine-rack in the larder. She didn't want him to see her eyes just now. He might accurately read the extent of her pain and bitterness, and it would be too degrading.

'White Bordeaux sounds fine. Shall we put some in the fridge to chill?'

'Yes. I'll do it.' She went to pass him to get to the fridge, and brushed against him as he moved the same way. Julius put a hand on her shoulder, and she froze, clutching the bottle of wine in front of her.

'Here, let me.' He took the bottle from her, put it in the fridge, and turned back to her. 'Sit down a moment, Victoria.'

She sat down obediently at the table, eyeing him warily, and Julius sat in the chair opposite, the pale eyes intent on her face.

'This isn't easy for me, either,' he said, in a low voice. 'If acting's not your strong point, grovelling isn't mine.'

'Nobody's asking you to grovel!' she burst out heatedly, but he shook his head, his eyes lidded and unreadable.

'No. Wrong word. I'm no good at this, Victoria. I'm very bad at apologising . . .'

'No apology needed either,' she cut in stiffly, gripping her hands into tense fists in her lap. 'Never apologise, never explain—isn't that the motto? I never used to approve of it, but now it strikes me as a good saying.'

'Nevertheless, I do have some explaining to do, and you're not making it easy for me.'

'Why? Why do you need to explain anything? You never pretended any feelings for me, Julius. Why pretend any now?'

Julius stood up abruptly, thrusting his hands into his pockets, and glaring down at the chair he had just vacated.

'Are you saying you feel nothing at all now, Victoria?'

'Feel nothing at all? Oh, no, I feel great love for my baby son, and great pride in my farm.'

'For me,' Julius interrupted stiffly. 'What are your feelings towards me?'

She took an unsteady breath. 'To be honest . . . I don't know. Indifference might be the most accurate description.' Her heart was thudding so loudly she was terrified he would hear it. She shrugged, and stood up, to try to lessen the acute stress she was feeling.

Julius made a sudden, wry face, and gave a twisted smile.

'Indifference is very negative. Could you work towards casual friendship? That might be a slightly more promising starting-point.'

'For what purpose?'

'If we're going to have any kind of partnership, we're going to need more than mutual indifference to make it work.'

'But we're not going to have any kind of partnership,' she snapped, pushed beyond her limits. 'What on earth makes you think that?'

'We have a son, Victoria,' said Julius, his tone ominously quiet. 'We are his parents. We need to work out some sort of arrangement.'

'Good lord! Doesn't adolescent infatuation blind people to the realities! Eighteen months ago, I thought you were cold, withdrawn, repressed, aggressive . . . but calf-love definitely blinded me to your insufferable pomposity.'

Julius said nothing, and her outburst hung in the air, echoing around the silent kitchen. There was a muscle twitching in Julius's cheek, but his face was deadpan, and she had no way of knowing if her words had amused or infuriated him.

He turned away and opened the Aga, and extracated the *gratin* dish. A delicious smell wafted out at her.

'This is ready. Where shall we eat it?'

She hesitated. 'There's a fire burning in the sitting-room, we could eat it there if you don't mind eating off a tray.'

Julius shook his head. 'We'll eat off trays,' he agreed firmly, gathering wine, cutlery and plates as she handed them out, and following her down to the sitting-room at the front of the farmhouse.

Flames from the logs were throwing shadows over the beamed walls, reflecting in the rows of pictures and on the glossy dark oak furniture. Victoria switched on lights, and the eerie, other-worldly atmosphere disappeared at once. It was a large, square sitting-room, with pale green carpet and flowery pink and green upholstery, with french doors which led out on to the walled garden. It was south-facing, light and sunny in the summer, and warm in the winter. One, of her favourite rooms.

A two-seater sofa stood parallel with the fire, and self-consciously Victoria avoided it, sitting instead in the small Queen Anne chair by the fire. Julius sat in the deeper armchair on the other side. She was briefly reminded of the way her parents used to sit in the same positions, and fought off the familiar wave of sadness, tinged with bitterness. She had made a discovery about her parents' relationship while her father had been ill in hospital, and she had been searching for the missing pieces of bird china, and she had never been able to think of them in quite the same way again.

'I know I've said this before, but I was very sorry to hear about your father's death,' said Julius, pouring wine into two glasses and handing one to her. 'Was it very sudden?'

'He—he was ill for about six weeks. In hospital for three.' She stopped, suddenly aware of the coincidence of Julius's question. Had he read her mind?

She lowered her eyes, anxious to change the subject.

'The Mildred Butler fetched a good price, didn't it?'

'A crazy price,' Julius agreed. 'I was in New York when it was auctioned, and of course an American bought it.'

'I remember you said they were very keen on that kind of thing in America.'

'Yes. You say you couldn't find any more of the creamware?'

'No. I hunted just about everywhere. When Dad went into hospital the financial situation was pretty desperate, but I didn't find any.' Instead, she found her father's letters from his mistress, she added silently, aware that Julius was watching her intently.

'But you did find something which upset you,' Julius prompted perceptively. 'What was it, Victoria? I had the feeling something was wrong when we were talking about it at De Lembers.'

'Oh, nothing much, really. I just found out my father had been having an affair,' she said lightly, with a casual shrug. 'There were loads of letters hidden in the back of an old sideboard. I suppose in these days of one-in-three divorces, it's quite unrealistic to imagine any married couple remain faithful to each other for very long.'

Julius said nothing, but watched her face thoughtfully. When the silence stretched out, she felt compelled to continue. 'The letters were from a woman called Joanie. They dated back to when I was about fifteen. The funny thing was when I read them I understood all sorts of things. Times when Dad had missed my school play, or my birthday party. Things like that. It's amazing how naïve ou can be, isn't it?'

'Did you talk to your father about the letters?'

'Hardly—he was lying in a hospital bed. He was dying.' She stopped, aware of a shake creeping back into her voice and anxious to disguise it. Julius sat forward on his chair, his eyes suddenly glitteringly angry.

'You've had a rough time, Victoria,' he said at last, his voice abrupt. 'I'm sorry——'

'Oh, don't be! I'll survive.' To her horror, the throw-away tone she had begun cracked into a half-sob, and tears welled in her eyes, stinging and hot. She turned her face away, and dashed a hand across her eyes, but this time she couldn't stem the flood. She began to sob and she couldn't stop herself.

'Victoria——' Julius was in front of her, taking her into his arms and holding her there, tight against him, even though she stayed stiff and unyielding.

'I'm sorry, I don't know what's the matter with me,' she choked, muffled against his shirt.

'It's all right. This is supposed to do you good,' Julius said, on a wry note. 'Though I'll confess the sound of a woman crying always makes we want to run a mile.'

She extricated herself, and glared at him through her tears.

'No one's stopping you,' she said shakily.

'I'm sorry. Don't take offence again. I'm just trying to be honest,' he amended, ruefully. 'Here.' He took a clean white handkerchief from his pocket and she accepted it silently, scrubbing her face with it and blowing her nose.

Julius sat back and took a drink of wine.

'So far your experience of life hasn't been too good, then,' he murmured thoughtfully. 'You were brave enough to attempt a relationship with me, and I let you down badly, didn't I? And then you found out that relationships are hardly worth the pain of bothering because even your own father was cheating. Is that it?'

She shrugged, eyeing him coldly. 'Don't try and patronise me, Julius,' she snapped, back in control again. She screwed the white handkerchief into a ball between her fists, and drew a deep breath. 'Whatever my philosophy is these days, it's really no business of yours.'

'Whatever you say,' he said, at last.

She stared at the fire, her emotions in turmoil. Just now, his touch had been ecstasy. The knowledge that he still had the power to arouse her was like a knife through her chest. For a few moments she hated him so intensely all pretence at indifference evaporated.

'Shall we eat some of this before it gets cold?' Julius suggested levelly, and she nodded wordlessly, bending to spoon some out and handing a plate to Julius without meeting his eyes.

'It's very good,' she said politely, when she had eaten a few mouthfuls. In fact it was superb, but she had no inclination to heap praise on his head just now. 'Is this your party piece, or do you have a wide repertoire of clever supper dishes?'

'I do a few vegetarian versions of this. Apart from that

I cook mainly in a wok. I can concoct quite interesting things with shellfish and vegetables and garlic and ginger.'

'That sounds . . . different, anyway.' She smiled involuntarily. 'Personally I prefer Italian food to Chinese—lasagne followed by chocolate roulade.'

'Rather rich for my taste,' Julius countered gravely.

'I remember. You suffer from indigestion,' Victoria said, with an innocent smile. 'How is your digestion these days?'

'My digestion is perfect,' said Julius drily. 'Ever since I resigned from De Lembers' Board.'

'Is that why you resigned? Was the job too stressful or something?'

Julius poured some more wine. He gazed into his glass, and the firelight reflected in his eyes.

'Maybe. It's hard to know where to start to explain it to you.'

Victoria put her empty plate down on the hearth with a clatter, and threw another log on to the fire. The flames began to lick and flicker around it, and when Julius lifted his eyes and looked intently at her, there were twin flames in the silver.

'You don't have to explain it to me. It's none of my business.'

'Yes, it is. Meeting you, going to New York, and what happened over there—they're linked. I want to explain why I went in the first place.'

'You had to investigate a fraud, you said.'

'Yes. But if there hadn't been a fraud to investigate, I would have gone anyway. I was ambitious. New York office was the logical next step. I was in line for the chairmanship if things went right. New York was the final attempt to prove to myself that my life was going the way I wanted it to go.'

Victoria kept her eyes on the fire. Her throat tightened but she managed to keep her voice detached.

'But it didn't?'

'It proved the opposite,' said Julius, with a note of self-mockery. 'There was a man called Samuel Rochas working in our New York office. He was a very old friend of mine. We grew up together for a few years—he was the son of one of my foster-families. We kept in touch after I went back to the childrens' home. Sam had devoted his whole life to creating a powerful, materialistic empire round himself. Money and power. They'd taken the place of personal relationships. He was divorced from his wife, he hardly saw his children. He didn't even care. All he cared about was making money.'

'And he was the one involved in the fraud?' Victoria said with a twisted smile.

'Yes.'

'And you had to expose him.'

'Yes. The whole edifice crumbled round him. He'd got nothing. No job, no power, no friends, and no family. He tried to kill himself.'

'You must have felt terrible.'

'I felt like a Judas,' Julius agreed drily. 'But the worst thing was seeing myself in him.'

He looked at her frankly, and the vulnerability in his eyes briefly touched a chord buried inside her.

'You mean, there but for the grace of God went you?'

'Slightly ungrammatical, but yes. I think that is what I felt.'

'Surely resigning from the board was a drastic step,' she reasoned, struggling to remain impartial, to show no personal involvement. 'You don't mean you were involved in fraud as well?'

'No. Of course not.'

'Then why resign? A minor adjustment in priorities would have sufficed.'

'Possibly. Except that I'd already been struggling with a major adjustment in priorities. Ever since a weekend in

Warwickshire when a stunning red-haired eighteen-year-old flung herself into my bed.'

Heat rushed to her face. 'I did not fling myself into your bed!' she protested hotly. 'I . . . I came to your room to apologise and . . . you grabbed me!'

Julius gazed at her levelly, and a glimmer of amusement showed in the silver stare. 'I don't recall you putting up much of a fight,' he said gently.

Victoria stood up abruptly. 'Do you want anything else to eat? There are some chocolate cakes I baked this afternoon, or I've got some fruit.'

'Fruit, please.' Julius's voice was drily amused.

'Fine. I'll make some coffee as well.' She took the dishes with her, and closed the door on him, storming down the passage to the kitchen, uncaring whether she dropped anything or not. How could he be so . . . callous? Taunting her about that weekend?

She collected a basket of fruit, a chocolate cake for herself, and made a pot of strong Nescafé with barely restrained violence. He was an insufferable egotist. He couldn't resist gloating over that past conquest. She strode back with the tray, still seething with fury.

'There are pears and oranges,' she said tersely, putting the basket in front of Julius with scant grace. She poured coffee and retreated to her chair in stiff silence.

'I'm sorry, Victoria,' said Julius, peeling a pear with precision. 'I didn't intend to upset you again. But it's difficult to pretend none of it happened. Particularly with Charles's existence.'

She glared at him challengingly. 'Julius, let's get one thing straight. Charles is my child. It took nine long months for him to develop. In my body. After just one night, not even that, a few moments only, you ceased to be involved in the process. So please don't think you have any rights or interest in my son!'

Her voice was shaking, and she stopped abruptly. Julius had stopped eating the pear, and had grown very still. The level penetrating stare he returned gradually began to unnerve her.

'I didn't exactly rape you that night, Victoria,' he said sardonically. 'You were touchingly eager to let me take your virginity. Knowing you had taken no precautions against pregnancy. It seems to me that I have every right to declare an interest in our son.'

Victoria stood up. She was dimly aware that this conversation was getting them nowhere, that they had somehow strayed from logic to blind emotion, but she was past caring.

'Will you please go?' she said quietly. 'If it will keep you away from me, I'll arrange for you to see Charles quite regularly. But I don't want you to come here again.'

Julius rose to his feet in a fluid, powerful movement, and the pale, lidded gaze was so scathing she longed to drop her eyes under the onslaught. Only pride and fury kept them level.

'I'll go,' he said tautly, 'but not before I've proved that you're lying to me and to yourself.'

Before she could duck him, he had pulled her into his arms. He controlled her furious struggles with what seemed an almost inhuman strength. His fingers were hard as he twisted her chin up until her mouth was beneath his, and then he kissed her.

In the midst of her anger, Victoria felt a wave of despair. She knew that her body was going to betray her. She wanted to fight and struggle and scream, but instead she circled his neck with her arms and ran her fingers into his short blond hair, pulling his mouth down harder on her own and returning the kiss with a passion she had forgotten she was capable of feeling.

When their lips parted for a moment she drew in a breath

that sounded like a sob, but her whole body was on fire, as if all her anger and resentment were transformed into heightened sexual desire.

'Oh, Julius, please, please,' she heard herself whispering against his mouth, as her body strained towards him.In response he swung her into his arms and took her to the sofa in front of the fire, trapping her on his lap as he kissed her more deeply. Victoria couldn't think any more. All she wanted was to be closer, to surrender to this limp, melting feeling in her bones, and this fiery ache in her stomach. Her struggles to escape had changed to struggles to be as close to Julius as possible, and with a groan he pushed her full length on the sofa and responded to her urgent movements by flicking open the buttons on her blouse, and unzipping her skirt to slide it down her legs. He encountered the cameo brooch and she lay in trembling impatience while he carefully unhooked it, and laid it on the low table beside them. Then at last she felt his lips on her throat, and his hands could part the silk covering of her blouse and expose her breasts to receive the caresses they ached for.

She gave a choked cry of pleasure as she felt his tongue on her hardened nipples, and he drew back for a moment, his face shadowy and almost unrecognisable above her, the pupils dilated with desire.

'Oh, Victoria,' he breathed unevenly, following the path of his mouth with his fingers, peeling the black tights from the silken plane of her stomach and sending another convulsion of pleasure through her. 'If you only knew how much I've longed to do this to you again.'

Somehow, through the mists of arousal, his words seemed to strike home. Reality came crashing back to her, and she froze beneath his stroking hands, finding the necessary strength to resist her own treacherous response to him.

'No, no!' she managed to say, pushing him away and curling herself up into a protective ball. She didn't want to be an object to Julius, someone he 'did things to'. She wasn't going to be treated as a quick, easy lay by a man who didn't love her, even if he did have the power to arouse her to mindless desire. She didn't trust him, she couldn't trust him. She would never trust another man again.

Julius had slid to kneel on the floor beside her, and was watching her intently, his breathing slightly erratic but his eyes level and unwavering, rather as a cat watches a mouse.

'Now I suppose you're going to say you weren't enjoying that?' he said finally, raising an eyebrow tauntingly.

'Please go,' she told him, in a muffled voice. 'There's no point even trying to explain. Just go.'

He knelt there for a while, appearing stunned, then at last he straightened up effortlessly and bent to gather up the remains of their supper things from the hearth.

'Thanks for supper,' he said, briefly, and carried the tray back to the kitchen while she stayed huddled at the end of the sofa, clutching her skirt around her, hardly daring to move. Her hair had escaped from its tight pleat during their frenzied lovemaking, and she wound a long curl repeatedly round her finger as she hugged her knees.

She heard Julius's footsteps returning down the passage, and she held her breath. But he didn't come back to say goodbye. The front door opened and closed, and after a few minutes she heart the low roar of the Mercedes pulling out of the courtyard and receding into the distance as it disappeared down the lane from the farm.

CHAPTER SEVEN

VICTORIA was deeply asleep when the telephone rang, and for a few moments she struggled to shake free from a vivid, muddled dream. But Julius's harsh voice brought her abruptly back to reality.

'Victoria? I'm sorry, I've just realised how early it is.' He sounded weary, with a trace of self-mockery. 'I couldn't sleep,' he added, by way of explanation.

Propping herself up on her elbow, she glanced at the bedside clock in angry disbelief.

'It's half past five in the morning, Julius!' she said coldly, stiffening as last night's intimacy came flooding back. 'Where are you? Back in London?'

'No, I'm still at the Golden Lion. Look Victoria, after last night I . . .'

'I don't want to talk about it,' she cut in awkwardly, 'And there's no need to apologise. It was just as much my fault.' Heat coursed through her again as she remembered her passionate response. How could she have let it happen?

The silence stretched on, and she found herself wondering wearily why she could have thought Julius would bow to her wishes and leave her in peace. When he had walked out last night, she'd had a wild idea he might disappear again, and the prospect had brought a kind of agonised relief.

'I'm sorry I woke you,' he said finally, jolting her out of her brooding thoughts, 'I'm not thinking too straight at the moment. But I've got to see you again, Victoria. Today.'

'Today? Julius, I've got a lot of work to do. I'm sure you must have as well.' Panic was rising at the prospect of seeing him again so soon. Her voice rose slightly. 'Can't you give me a breathing space?'

'I want to see Charles again,' he said bleakly. 'He's my son, Victoria. I've seen him for a total of ten minutes.'

Victoria hesitated, gripping the receiver so tightly her knuckles were white. Then she expelled her breath in defeat. Defensiveness and resentment towards Julius couldn't change a simple truth. He was Charles's father, and he had a right to get to know his son. That was an irrefutable fact among a seething mass of doubts and fears which she was suddenly too weary to analyse.

'All right. If that's what you want,' she told him slowly, her voice cool. 'I'll see you later, then.'

'Maybe we could go to the park, feed the ducks, or something.'

'Just as you like.' She replaced the receiver carefully, and lowered herself back on to the bed, feeling emotionally exhausted, but after a few moments, she sat up again. She might as well get up, there was no chance of getting back to sleep now. And if she made an early start to the day's chores, Julius's visit wouldn't throw her quite so far behind. She slowly showered, and brushed her red curls until they shone in a heavy cloud around her shoulders, then dragged on faded denims and an oversize peach and white angora sweater which reached to mid-thigh. A brief glance in the mirror showed the ravages of a restless night. She looked pale and heavy-eyed. She brushed some blusher lightly over her cheekbones, then added a couple of tortoiseshell combs to hold her hair back from her face.

Then, hearing Charles rattling the various toys in his cot, she went to greet him, feeling the dark cloud lifting slightly in anticipation of seeing his toothless smile of welcome.

'Hello there, my poppet,' she smiled, lifting him out and hugging the soft, warm body against her. It was impossible to remain tense and miserable when she held her baby son in her arms. Holding him a few inches away from her, she examined him with a critical grin.

'You're beautiful, but we'd better tidy you up. You've got your Daddy coming to see you again this morning!'

Once she had said it aloud, it seemed easier to accept. The day ahead no longer seemed quite so intolerable. She even hummed under her breath while she changed Charles's nappy and washed his face and hands, and dressed him in his smartest red towelling jumper with a picture of an apple on the front, and wriggled him into denim dungarees.

'There, you look very handsome,' she told him solemnly, as they went in search of breakfast. With Charles safely strapped in his high-chair she made toast for herself and boiled an egg for Charles to squash toast soldiers into. He had just managed to coat his face with yolk and flick half the soldiers on to the floor for Rough to eat when Julius appeared at the kitchen door.

She was taken by surprise, and felt furious at the flutter of apprehension and excitement which cramped her stomach at the sight of him standing there in the doorway. He looked paler than usual beneath his tan and the white-blond hair was slicked back damply, as if he had just had a shower. His pallor seemed to exaggerate the gaunt hollowness of his cheeks and the shadowed sockets of his eyes. She wanted to rush over and throw her arms around him, but pride kept her rooted to the spot.

'Good morning,' he said quietly, his eyes flicking over the domestic scene. 'Am I in time for breakfast?'

'I should think so. What do you want?'

'Do you have any muesli?' His face was unsmiling, but as he glanced at Charles she saw a warmth in his eyes she could swear he had never used towards her. She produced the bag of muesli and a dish and spoon, and plonked them down on the table rather abruptly.

'Thank you. I'd love some black coffee, if you're making some.'

Shrugging off his Barbour, he sat down at the oak table and began tipping muesli into the bowl.

'There's coffee in the pot over there. Help yourself.'

He glanced up at her, suddenly appearing aware of her irritation, and raking a hand through his damp hair he flashed one of his devastating rueful grins. She felt the usual maddening struggle . . . Julius's smile was so rare, so potent, it was almost impossible to resist. Staring back at him silently, she tried to remain detached, but it was difficult not to think how beautiful he looked, just in simple grey cords and a thick, checked shirt.

'I'm sorry. I wasn't intending to demand waitress service,' he said softly. 'I'm feeling rough this morning, that's all. I drank too much malt whisky last night, and then I couldn't even sleep it off.'

She swallowed hard. How charming he could be when he bothered to try, she thought cynically, slapping butter on her toast with more force than necessary. 'More fool you,' she remarked tartly, 'I thought you always drank in moderation!'

'So did I.' There was a dry note in his voice, and catching his eye she reddened involuntarily. The implication was fairly clear. The frustration of last night had driven him to hit the bottle.

Deciding silence was the wisest response, she watched him devour a huge dish of muesli and drink two cups of coffee, thinking how odd it felt, sitting here eating breakfast with Julius and Charles. Such a false impression of domesticity. As if they were a happy family.

'Feeling better?' she asked casually, as Julius leaned back and stretched wearily.

'Yes, thank you.' His eyes lingered on her face for a few moments as if he was about to say more, but then he turned to smile at Charles, laughing at the eggy face which beamed back at him.

'And how are you this morning?' he enquired solemnly. 'I can see you're enjoying that egg, although you're having some difficulty locating your mouth, by the look of things. And I'll bet you hate being cleaned up. Correct?'

Charles responded with the impressive stream of babble he used to communicate with, and Julius grinned, picking up the discarded spoon and offering more egg, which was impatiently thrust to the floor.

'No more egg. Right, I understand,' Julius agreed gravely, and Victoria shook her head reprovingly.

'It's very rude to throw your breakfast on the floor,' she lectured Charles, handing a damp sponge to Julius to use on the baby's face while she wiped the floor. She braced herself for the usual screaming session which accompanied face-wiping, and straightened in astonishment when it didn't materialise, to see Charles gurgling with apparent delight as Julius carefully sponged off the food around his mouth. She gazed at them both helplessly. It was unbelievable. The attraction between father and son was so potent, it was almost blinding. She watched as Julius lifted Charles out of the chair and swung him up into the air, laughing while the child giggled appreciatively.

'How did you do that?' she demanded finally, half laughing. 'He always screams when I wipe his face.'

'My lethal charm?' Julius suggested blandly, tucking the child on his hip with such practiced confidence she frowned at him curiously.

'You seem very relaxed with babies.'

Julius looked vaguely surprised. 'Do I? I suppose it's because years ago we had a rota at the children's home. The older kids took turns to look after the little ones.' He grinned at her astonished expression. 'Maybe that accounts for it. Women don't have a monopoly on baby psychology, do they?'

'No. And I'm impressed,' she admitted, laughing slightly. 'I don't think Andrew knows one end of Jonathan from the other!'

Julius was about to say something when Elspeth appeared in the doorway, yawning widely, in a lacy cotton housecoat which she grabbed round herself in confusion when she saw Julius.

'Oh! Good morning!' she exclaimed, blushing beetroot as she looked from one to the other. 'I didn't realise . . . I mean, I thought you'd gone.'

Victoria came to her rescue.

'It's all right, Elspeth. Julius did go last night, but he came back early this morning,' she said blandly, determined to put the record straight. She didn't want Elspeth under the impression they had had a passionate reconciliation.

'Oh, don't worry about me, don't feel you have to explain,' the Scottish girl beamed, clearly not believing a word. 'I'll just pop back upstairs and get dressed, since we've company for breakfast.'

Victoria watched her go in exasperation, seeing from Julius's expression that he was enjoying the irony of the situation.

'I find myself wishing Elspeth's fantasies were reality,' he said in a low voice, and before she could sidestep he had slid his free hand around the back of her neck, under the weight of her hair, and taken possession of her softly parted lips, his tongue exploring the shape of her mouth, and then probing inside and hungrily deepening the kiss until she was trembling and helpless. With a slight, violent twist of her head she freed herself, glaring at him furiously, breasts heaving as she fought for control.

'They're not reality, and never will be,' she whispered scorchingly, holding out her arms for Charles and cradling the firm little body against her breasts.

'No?' He sounded sardonic again. 'But when I kiss you, Victoria, you seem to be saying something quite different.'

The silver gaze held her motionless for a few seconds and then she dropped her eyes evasively, abruptly changing the oppressive atmosphere by tickling Charles under his chin and laughing back as he responded.

Julius didn't pursue his theory, to her relief, and for the rest of the day they enjoyed Charles together, taking him to the park where Julius pushed him high on the babyswings and carried him to the top of the big slide while she held her breath apprehensively. They fed the ducks, demonstrating the technique to Charles and then laughing at his comical expression when the crumbs he threw were caught in the wind and blown back in his face. The sun was shining, and Victoria began to relax more with Julius than she had ever managed before. He seemed genuinely interested in her lifestyle, her routines with Charles, and she even found herself telling him about her pregnancy, hiding a slight embarrassment behind a flippant façade.

'It needn't follow you'd have the same problems again,' he told her quietly, concern in his eyes when she admitted Charles had been delivered by forceps and considered lucky to escape brain damage.

'Really? How would you know?' she countered coolly.

'I read a couple of books on the subject, when I found out about the baby,' he said, with a twist of a smile. She was dumbfounded, and then found herself laughing. The idea of Julius reading baby books seemed highly improbable, and somehow very funny. When she had sobered, she said seriously, 'I doubt if there'll be a next time.'

Julius took hold of her shoulders, forcing her to look at him.

'Why? You're young, and you're wonderful with Charles. Surely you'd like more children?'

'What has that got to do with you?' she enquired calmly, raising her eyebrows. His face tautened under her mocking gaze, and he gave her a slight shake, the grey eyes hardening.

'Victoria, tell me how I can get through to you,' he demanded, harsh urgency in his voice. His touch, and the appeal in his eyes, sent shivers of longing down her back, but she had a steely grip on her emotions.

'You could try opening up a bit,' she suggested lightly, twisting out of his hands. 'Giving away a little information about yourself. I recall you had an aversion to talking about yourself. Like trying to prise open a clam!'

There was a long pause. They walked on, along the river bank, Charles safely on his reins toddling between them. She had a feeling Julius was conducting the old internal battle with himself. Finally, he glanced sideways at her, his face rueful.

'All right.' He sounded like a criminal up for interrogation, she thought with a stab of amusement. 'What do you want to know?'

'Mmm, let's see. Your mysterious childhood, for a start.'

'Fair enough.' Julius seemed to tense up, somehow, but he continued evenly. 'My mother was Danish. I never met my father but I believe he was English. When I was five I went to live with foster-parents, but . . . '

'Why? What happened to your mother?'

Glancing at his profile, she felt her heart go out to him suddenly. The harsh face of the man seemed only just to disguise the anguish of the child he had once been.

'She married someone,' he said finally. 'Some man who didn't want another man's child messing things up.'

She drew in her breath, pity welling up inside her. 'Go on,' she said quietly.

He shot a swift, mocking glance at her.

'It doesn't get any better. After two or three sets of foster-parents, I spent the rest of the time in a children's home. Left school at fifteen, and helped on a junk stall in a market in Bermondsey. He smiled slightly, adding, 'That was the start of my career. I had entrepreneurial skills I never realised before, I learned to recognise valuable pieces among the piles of rubbish. I never looked back, as they say.'

'Did you never see your mother again?' she interrupted, finding it impossible to believe any mother could simply hand her child over to foster-parents to please a prospective husband.

'Yes. I saw her again when I was seven. She wanted me back.' His voice was expressionless, but there was a glitter in his eyes, hard as stones in the sunlight. Victoria shivered.

'But you didn't go back?'

'No. I didn't go back.'

'Why? Oh, Julius, why?' The picture was so bleak and bereft, she could hardly bear to imagine it.

He shrugged, his smile harder. 'I just wasn't a very cooperative child, I suppose.' He stopped for a moment, as if he was trying to get the past into perspective. 'I don't like talking about this. I think that's because, looking back, I can see that I must have wanted to go back to my mother more than anything else in the world. I have memories of my first five years with her, strange as it may seem. A lot of happy memories. Blurred sort of images of someone very warm. But I suppose she must have been a very mixed-up woman.' He shook his head, with a short laugh. 'At the time, though, I took exception to being shunted around.'

'But surely, at seven . . . I mean, how come you had any choice?'

The silver gaze was bleak and mocking. 'The social services of the day had never heard a child scream and yell for quite so long, as I dimly recall. They eventually advised my mother to leave me where I was. She went back to Denmark with her new husband. She's dead now, I discovered recently.'

It was the saddest story Victoria had ever heard. Sympathy welled up but she sensed Julius would reject it.

'Why didn't you stay with your foster-parents? Why go back to the children's home?'

'If your face doesn't fit, you're out,' Julius shrugged. 'Foster-parents are under no obligation to keep you. It's not like adoption.'

She stared down at the top of Charles's head, struggling with her painful reactions. If you had a childhood like that, did you put up barricades? Did you maybe find it hard to trust people, hard to risk letting your feelings show? She had no idea. Her own childhood had been secure, loving, happy, and above all trusting. Her first cruel lesson, taught to her by Julius, had come much too late. And then her father, indirectly, had taught her the second.

'Well?' she said brightly, determined to hide her emotions. 'Is that it? How about romantic involvements?' She had a masochistic urge suddenly, driving her to add, 'Hayley told me once you'd broken more hearts than she'd eaten take-away pizzas.'

The grey eyes were quizzical. 'I've known several women, obviously. I'm nearly thirty-two. I doubt if I've broken their hearts, however.'

She looked at him witheringly. If he only knew the effect of those eyes . . . Hayley was right. Julius was dangerously attractive to women, even more so because he seemed unaware of the devastation he left behind, once he detached himself and moved on.

'Yes, I see,' she smiled. 'So never get involved—is that your motto?'

'Possibly. But up to eighteen months ago, I'd never met anyone I wanted to get seriously involved with.'

She stiffened, trying to assimilate this. What was he saying? For a wild, crazy moment, she thought he was talking about her. Then common sense saved her. Julius wouldn't insult her intelligence now by trying to pretend he had found her irresistible all this time! Particularly since he hadn't even bothered to contact her until just over a week ago.

A sick feeling came over her as his real meaning sank in. Poor Julius. What a dilemma to find himself in when he came back from America. And no wonder he had been so reluctant to respond to her soulful gazes and clumsy adoration, that fateful weekend at Hayley's. He had met someone who meant something to him, someone he could trust, and then he had had to endure a weekend of earth-shattering boredom with a love-struck adolescent! What a complete fool she had made of herself.

'Shall we go back?' she asked, evading Julius's curious gaze. 'It's turning colder.'

'Victoria? Don't shut me out.' His voice was low and compelling, and she swung away from him angrily.

'Why not? It's a trick I learned from you,' she said brightly, walking back towards the park.

He caught up in a few swift strides, lifting Charles to sit on his shoulders and instantly producing gurgles of happiness.

'Look, maybe we've both had changes of heart over the last year and a half,' he said tautly. 'But Charles is our joint responsibility now. At least give me a chance, Victoria!'

She was hardly listening. The numb misery inside her was expanding, and guilt along with it. It had suddenly occurred to her that through her impulsive infatuation that weekend, she had probably caused more trouble and upheaval in Julius's life than he had in her own.

She sat stiffly in the back of the Mercedes on the way back to the farm, Charles on her lap, her heart leaden with misery. What a ghastly shock for Julius, to find that a girl he had slept with once, just one night, had borne him a baby son, and a new sort of responsibility entirely had been thrust on him. Outside the farm, she climbed out of the car with Charles in her arms.

'It's been a lovely day out,' she said politely, 'but do you mind if I don't ask you in now? Charles is sleepy, and I've got a lot of work to catch up with.'

Julius was scanning her face, uncharacteristically confused.

'Victoria, I have to fly to Milan tomorrow. There's an art collection I've been invited to value. Will you come with me?'

She felt her jaw drop, then gathered her wits quickly.

'I couldn't possibly. Thanks anyway. I've got the farm to run and Charles to look after.'

'There's Elspeth. Or you could bring him with you. I'd like that.'

She shook her head decisively. 'Sorry. It's out of the question.'

'Then I'll see you at the weekend,' he said quietly, his expression darkening as she continued to shake her head.

'I've got some old university friends coming to stay,' she told him calmly. 'So I'll be busy. Uncle Sebastian's coming to see you, Charles!' she added, bouncing the baby in her arms, keeping her eyes anywhere but on Julius's tense face.

'Sebastian?' His tone was grim enough to make her back

away from him, but she nodded blithely.

'An old friend. He's doing his Ph.D. in Manchester at the moment. We keep in touch. He's been very supportive.

There was a stony silence, and then Julius said hoarsely,

'That's a pity. I was going to ask you and Charles to drive back to London with me on Saturday afternoon. There's a charity auction dinner at the Hurlingham Club. I was hoping you'd come with me . . .'

'Oh, that's a shame. Still, no doubt you'll find someone else to take.'

She feared for a moment that Julius was going to explode in a rare show of anger, but controlling his feelings with visible effort he turned away to the car.

'Have a good trip to Milan,' she called after him casually. 'Ring me next week some time.'

'You can depend on it,' he said caustically, climbing into the Mercedes and accelerating away with an angry crunch of gravel.

She stood on the doorstep, watching the car disappearing down the lane, and realising that tears were running down her cheeks.

She dashed a hand impatiently over her face, and went inside. It was pointless crying over Julius. Crying solved nothing, and it certainly wouldn't wash away the past.

CHAPTER EIGHT

THE rest of that week passed in a nightmare of pretending everything was all right. Setting herself a punishing schedule, Victoria worked from dawn till night and collapsed into bed in exhaustion every evening.

By Friday she was almost on her knees, but the prospect of her friends' visit seemed like a light at the end of a dark tunnel. The company of old friends was just what she needed. Her tangled problems with Julius could be forgotten. She could recall her happy student days, and relax.

But her friends were fascinated by Charles. He had grown so rapidly he was almost unrecognisable as the tiny baby they had last seen at the christening. Inevitably the conversation centred around Charles's engaging character, and the mystery of his absent father.

'He's so beautiful, Vicky! He takes after his father, presumably? In colouring, I mean.' Caroline, plump and blonde as ever, and in her final year of a drama degree, was the first one to pluck up courage to mention Julius. Watching Victoria building Lego towers for Charles to scatter gleefully across the carpet, she was shaking her head in admiration.

'It's a silly question really, since he's hardly a brown-eyed redhead like Victoria,' Shelley snapped, tossing back her dark hair scornfully.

'Well, I never met the infamous Mr Korda,' said Caroline, undaunted, 'but if his son's anything to go by he must be decidedly gorgeous, darling!'

Shelley was frowning. She had always been the serious one, although after getting a First in biology she had surprised them all by taking a job in a clothes boutique until the right job came along.

'It doesn't look to me as if Victoria wants to discuss him,' she advised solemnly. 'And if some guy put me in the family way and disappeared without a word I expect I'd feel the same.'

'Did he never come back?' Caroline pursued relentlessly, leaning back from the fire, her round cheeks scorched red from toasting another tea-cake. Tea-cakes round the fire had been a ritual delight since they had shared their rented house in Exeter.

'Oh, give it a rest, Caro!' Shelley said irritably.

'As a matter of fact,' stated Victoria carefully, spreading half an inch of butter on her tea-cake and avoiding everyone's eyes, 'he did come back. A couple of weeks ago.'

Caroline's eyes grew rounder. 'He did? Darling, how wonderfully romantic!' she breathed theatrically. 'And did he know about baby Charles?'

'Oh, yes, that's the only reason he showed up again. I think he feels a sense of responsibility for his baby son.'

She found it almost impossible to keep the bitterness from oozing through between every word.

'So what's his story?' Shelley demanded bluntly, her mouth full of tea-cake, black brows drawn together in a fierce frown. Victoria poured more tea, outwardly unperturbed, aware that Sebastian was gazing moodily into the fire, deliberately not taking part in this conversation. 'Where the hell has he been all this time?'

'New York. And don't sound so indignant on my behalf, Shelley,' Victoria laughed, sipping her tea with a slightly unsteady hand. 'Just one night doesn't entitle a woman to the remainder of a man's life, you know. I was the fool. He was the honest one.

'So what does he want? He's not trying to take Charles away from you?' Caroline exclaimed, turning pink with indignation.

'No, no. I don't think so.' Victoria's heart turned

cold at this suggestion. She was fairly certain Julius had no
such intention. But there again, she wasn't quite sure exactly
what he did want. Did he still have a relationship with this
woman he had fallen in love with? And if so, could he
possibly have some idea of taking Charles to live with them?
The thoughts whirled endlessly, torturing her, and as the
weekend progressed she withdrew more and more into a
quiet shell.

Sebastian appeared to be watching her with gathering
tension, like a man with something important to say who
doesn't know quite how to begin.

'I finish my Ph.D. course at the end of this year,' he
confided at last. 'One of my papers was very well received at
a conference in Mexico. They might even publish it. When I
get my doctorate, I can either look for a job in industry, or I
may be offered a research post in California.' He hesitated,
his blue eyes searching her face for response. 'It's a secure
position. The money's not as good as in industry, but it
would be a good life out there. If you could stand the
suffocating academic life . . . ' Victoria was staring at him in
surprise. 'I'd love it if you and Charles came with me,' he
finished in a rush, flushing slightly.

She felt deeply touched. Sebastian had kept in constant
contact, admittedly, but in all the time they had known each
other he'd kissed her once or twice, but seemed to accept her
insistence on a platonic relationship. He had been one of
several men at university who'd tried to talk her into bed but
been rebuffed. Most of the others had been too offended to
pursue the friendship, but Sebastian had stayed impressively
loyal. He had asked her to marry him once before, when she
had first discovered she was pregnant. But she had put that
down to his chivalry. She'd never dreamt he might still feel
that way towards her.

'I'm terribly fond of you, Seb,' she told him softly, 'but
apart from anything else, I wouldn't want to leave
Roundbridge.'

'Don't say no finally. Think about it, Vicky,' he urged

persuasively. 'I've always wanted you. And you're a fool if you wait around any longer for that jut-jawed antiques guy to make up his mind what he wants!'

She stiffened and turned away. They were leaning on a gate at the end of Lower Cowdown, watching Caroline and Shelley feeding the angoras, hand in hand with Charles, with much giggling and horseplay. The wind was cool but there was more warmth in the sun. Spring felt closer, and she even felt slightly hot in her Arran sweater and waxed cotton jacket.

'It's not what he wants,' she said at last, her voice suddenly determined. 'It's what I want that matters. And what I want is to be left alone to get on with my life. Without the complication of men!'

Sebastian gazed at her gloomily. 'A boy needs a father,' he pointed out solemnly.

'Oh, don't you start! You're as bad as Hayley!'

'All right, but you shouldn't let one bad experience sour you towards all the other men you meet. You never used to generalise about the male sex quite so sweepingly.' He tried to smile, but made a bleak job of it.

She didn't answer, but in that moment she felt Sebastian had summed up her philosophy rather too accurately. Men, in her opinion, were a poor risk when it came to matters of the heart. Look at her own parents. Apart from Julius, it had been a shattering experience finding out about Dad's betrayal. She had felt it as a personal insult. Dad had deliberately jeopardised his marriage, and therefore his family life. She and Hayley had presumably been insufficient incentive to sustain a monogamous relationship with their mother. But then men were like that, she had long ago decided. They functioned differently, they weren't made to conceive babies, to seek security and fidelity with a life-partner.

The odd thing was that Hayley hadn't seen it like that. She wasn't sure yet whether her sister was a gullible idiot, or a wiser woman of the world. But of course Hayley had her marriage to Andrew to sustain her rosy view of men. She could afford to be generous.

When her friends had gone their separate ways on Sunday afternoon, she felt in need of her sister's cheerful good humour to snap her out of the bleak mood descending on her. Gathering an armful of Hayley's favourite herbs, she put them into a carrier-bag, and then strapping Charles into his buggy she set off to walk the familiar route into the village.

'You look ghastly!' Hayley announced, eyeing her up and down with an infuriatingly knowing air. 'You should have come up to London this weekend with Julius. We had a marvellous time last night.'

Victoria stared at her sister blankly.

'You've been up to London this weekend? You've been with Julius?'

'Mmm.' Hayley seemed to hesitate a moment, then smiled secretively, and tugged her arm. 'Come and see my new painting,' she urged.

Bewildered, Victoria left Charles to play with William and Jonathan under Sheila's watchful care, and followed Hayley into the sitting-room. An oil painting hung over the mantelpiece, and she stared at it hard for a few minutes, before the truth dawned on her. It was Hayley, so clever and subtle that the likeness gradually materialised before her eyes like a scene through mist.

'Very good,' she nodded approvingly. 'When did you find time to sit for it?'

'I didn't,' Hayley told her triumphantly. 'It's not me. Now would you say my hair was straight, or curly?'

Victoria stared at her sister uncomprehendingly, then turned back to the picture. A funny feeling tightened her throat. Hayley was right, the picture was of a woman with long, curly red hair, tumbling down over smooth, olive-skinned shoulders. The unique style and technique at first hid the true subject matter, giving an impression of random patterns in a subtle swirl of colour.

'Well? Surely you've realised? It's you, darling!'

'Yes, I can see that now.' Victoria's voice sounded strange, muffed, quite unlike er own.

'Julius painted it,' Hayley said unnecessarily. 'He finished it ages ago. I had the impression he was going to give it to you, but then changed his mind. So I persuaded him to sell it to me. I hope you don't mind. But it is good, don't you think?'

'Yes. It's good.' She carefully avoided her sister's eyes. 'Vaguely impressionist. So Julius has embarked on his artistic career. He didn't waste much time.'

'He's been painting on and off for years,' Hayley explained. 'His stuff sells for anything upwards of ten thousand pounds. What it is to have the right contacts!'

'True.' She supposed his contacts were the types who frequented receptions at De Lembers, and auction dinners at the Hurlingham Club. No wonder he could charge so much for his pictures, she thought acidly.

'So you went to this dinner at the Hurlingham Club?' she asked, annoyed with herself for her curiosity. 'Was this something to do with De Lembers?'

'Yes, Julius is a Vice-President of the Ski Club UK, and they'd taken over the club for this auction dinner to raise money for Dr Barnardo's Homes,' said Hayley, her brown gaze bright and alert on her sister's face. 'It was a joint production between the Ski Club and De Lembers—through their shared connection with Julius, I suppose.'

'Oh.' Victoria sought for something non-committal to say, but she was finding it hard to remain calm and uninterested. 'It sounds terribly glamorous! What did you wear?'

'That strapless copper taffeta creation we chose together that day in London, remember? And I had my hair all piled up like this.' Hayley's demonstration with her stick-straight mane made them both giggle.

'The men wore black tie. Julius looks positively lethal in

evening dress, darling!'

'I can imagine.' Victoria hesitated, feeling slightly sick but compelled to ask the question. 'I suppose he was with some fabulous blonde?' There was a give-away tremble in her voice, and Hayley glanced at her sharply.

'No, brunette actually. Susan Goodman, his secretary. She's rather stunning, white skin and black hair and a bright red dress.'

Her voice didn't sound at all like her own as she asked, 'Secretary? I thought he'd resigned from De Lembers. How come he still has a secretary?'

'I think Susan felt a conflict of loyalties when Julius resigned,' Hayley laughed. 'She decided to work part-time for him, at a slight drop in salary, I should think! What devotion!'

'Quite,' said Victoria acidly. 'Positively dog-like!'

Hayley ignored this piece of sarcasm, and went on to describe the young downhill skiers she had met, who were in hard training for the winter Olympics, but Victoria wasn't listening. She was discovering a vivid, pictorial imagination, and taking central place at the moment was an image of Julius, looking dangerously attractive in evening dress, dancing with a black-haired beauty in a red dress.

'Julius seems to be in great demand for private auctions,' Hayley was saying. 'He'd just flown back from Milan, where he valued some rich Englishman's hoard of paintings. I'd guess his desire to drop out and be less materialistic will be short-lived.'

'Yes, I expect you're right,' Victoria agreed woodenly, her eyes drawn involuntarily to the portrait. 'Poor Julius. Cursed with the Midas Touch!' Or more likely he had never had any intention of surrendering his previous life-style, she thought caustically. Leopards, as they said, rarely changed their spots.

But, try as she might to ignore it, the portrait seemed to haunt her. It confused her. Julius had been sufficiently indifferent to her to lose touch completely after that weekend together, a year and a half ago. And yet, he had thought enough about her to paint her portrait. Quite vividly, from memory. It didn't make sense. None of Julius's behaviour seemed to make sense.

Or maybe it did, recalling his story the other night, his experience in New York and the fate of his friend Samuel Rochas. That explained his new philosophy, she supposed. He had suddenly developed a social conscience. After years of ruthless ambition and the pursuit of power, he was seeking spiritual gratification.

She smiled to herself rather cynically. Lucky for him that he had stumbled on such a tailor-made means of saving his soul. He had accidentally fathered a baby son in his absence, and now he could qualify as a compassionate member of the human race by offering support and friendship to mother and child.

The paperwork on the desk in front of her in the farm office seemed a meaningless jumble suddenly, and she slammed her pen down so hard it fell apart in the middle, and the spring flew out. Julius was welcome to his charity dinners, and his receptions in London. He could raise all the money he liked for children's homes, but he needn't patronise her with this new-found Christian charity. He made no pretence of offering love. At least, he was sparing her that hypocrisy. But as far as she was concerned, he could spare her the rest as well.

She was still in this militant mood on Monday night, and each time the telephone rang she snatched it up to tell Julius exactly what she thought of him. But Julius didn't ring, and she went to bed that night in bitter satisfaction. Julius had promised to ring her after the weekend, and he hadn't bothered. Typical. Obviously his weekend with the devoted Susan had driven all his good, paternal intentions clean out of his mind for a while. It didn't surprise her. It just proved how right she was not to be taken in by his lethal charm.

Tuesday was the start of the two-day sale at Mount Cotmayton, in the Cotswolds. The day dawned brilliantly sunny, and Victoria grasped the opportunity to escape from the nerve-racking business of waiting for Julius's next move. Despatching Elspeth and Charles to Hayley's for the night, she threw her suitcase into the Range Rover, along with the Sothebys' catalogue, and with promises to ring from her hotel she drove off, feeling like a fugitive escaping from prison.

She cruised through the Warwickshire countryside with an involuntary lift of her spirits. The Roundbridge she left behind looked like a farm in a children's picturebook this morning, with rolling fields of young green corn, and the acid-yellow haze of rape seed. The walled garden was full of daffodils and tulips, where they bloomed early, sheltered from the icy April winds. It was impossible to remain sunk in depression when nature was preaching optimism. And she had put on a new spring outfit in honour of today's trip, a jade silk suit with a fitted peplum jacket and a brilliantly coloured silk blouse underneath, in cheerful jade, red and yellow. She had even applied gallons of hand-cream to her sore, wind-chapped hands, in obedience to Hayley's threats of beauty salons and health farms unless she took herself in hand and slowed the pace she was working at.

She stopped for lunch at a favourite pub on the brow of a hill, and ate a ploughman's and a chocolate gateau on the terrace overlooking the glorious misty sweep of the Cotswold valley below. Then she pressed on until she saw the signs marked 'Sale This Day' and finally saw Mount Cotmayton shimmering in distant sunshine, pure symmetry in ancient Cotswold stone. An enormous marquee had been erected on one of its sweeping lawns, and cars were parked everywhere, with a preponderance of Rollses, Porsches and BMWs.

Groups of elegantly clad people strolled around between the marquee and the big house, and Victoria felt glad she had made an effort to dress smartly. She had bought the suit in London with Hayley, and her soft leather boots were the same dusky-red as the blouse. With her hair confined in a loose topknot and some carefully applied make-up, she felt

almost a match for the soignée women eyeing catalogues
with unlimited credit at their disposal.

She browsed around the lots out of curiosity. Even though
she had come only for farm equipment, the treasures of the
old house were alluring. Priceless paintings, glossy antique
furniture, rooms full of books. She felt a touch of sadness as
she strolled round. It grieved her to see big old houses carved
up, their owners' possessions auctioned off. There, but for
her intervention, went Roundbridge farm, she thought, with
a glow of gratitude to the Urquhart trust fund which had
made it possible. At least her family home had been spared
this ignominious fate.

She was gazing at a Gainsborough portrait when she
heard a low, beautifully modulated voice behind her.

'This is the one!' It was a woman's voice, warm and
confident.

Victoria was about to turn round to glimpse its owner
when another voice answered, a deep, clipped voice which
made the prickles rise up on the back of her neck. She slowly
turned round to see Julius standing there, casual in silver-
green cords and a checked shirt, hands thrust in the pockets
of a sleeveless olive green waistcoat. At his side was an ivory-
skinned brunette, intimidatingly smart in a black designer
suit, with crimson lips and nails. They were looking at a
painting of what appeared to be Captain Hook, from *Peter
Pan*. It was too late to sneak out, Julius had seen her. He
looked grim, she thought nervously, almost too preoccupied
to listen as he politely introduced the dark-haired woman as
his secretary, Susan Goodman. Victoria already knew who
she was. Hayley's description of the girl at the charity
auction dinner had been accurate.

'Lovely to meet you. I've heard such a lot about you,'
Susan was enthusing, shaking hands with a lot more
sincerity than Victoria expected. 'I'm only Julius's part-time
secretary now, aren't I?' she added, smiling up at him. 'But
after years of secretarial mollycoddling I don't think he's
quite grasped the fact that I'm not at his beck and call from

eight a.m. until seven p.m. every single day. Honestly, he's dragged me down here at literally a moment's notice . . . '

'Susan, would you go across to the marquee and check what number they're on?' Julius cut in smoothly, watching the shapely figure disappear from the room without any particular expression on his face.

Then he turned back to gaze into Victoria's face, the lidded gaze unnervingly tense.

'Hayley said I'd find you here,' he said without preamble. 'I thought this might be a good place to meet on neutral ground.'

'Really? How lucky that you could combine the occasion with business, wasn't it!' she said coldly.

He kept his eyes evenly on hers. 'I see no crime in that. I have a client who collects Hodge paintings. This one has been valued at a fraction of its true price.' He shrugged, his eyes narrowing slightly. 'Did you enjoy your weekend with Sebastian?' he added quietly.

'Yes, very much, thanks. Did you enjoy your weekend with Susan?' she countered calmly. Her heart was pounding in her chest but she was determined to hide her agitation.

Julius frowned slightly. 'Susan came to the charity auction with me. That's all.'

She shrugged. 'I don't much care whether you took her to the charity auction or took her to bed,' she said, watching the colour drain from Julius's face with a slight twist of pain inside her.

'Don't you?' he asked bleakly. She didn't answer, and Julius let out his breath on a sharp sigh. 'What were you looking for here? Were you just browsing?'

'I'm looking for some farm equipment,' she answered politely.

'Ah, yes. A new disc harrow, something like that?'

There was a brief smile in his eyes, and she shrugged again. 'A baler, actually.'

'I see. You'll probably have to wait until tomorrow for the auction of the farm implements. Did you realise that?'

'I wasn't sure. I imagined that might be the case. I'm staying overnight in Broadway.' She stopped, furious with herself for telling him this, but Julius appeared to know already.

'At the Southleache. Right?'

'Yes, but . . .'

'I'll see you there at eight,' he said quietly. 'And no running away, Victoria. We've got to talk.'

She was about to protest when Susan reappeared, gliding efficiently up to join them, with a slightly patronising smile at Victoria.

'Ten to go,' she announced in a low voice, 'and I think I saw Douglas Mindell from Christie's in the crowd, so there might be more competition than you think.'

The slender white hand with the crimson tips lingered for a few seconds longer than necessary on Julius's brown forearm, and Victoria looked away. Images of Julius in evening clothes dancing with the lady in red returned to twist a knife in her heart.

'Well, I think I'll stroll round and see if I come across the farm implements,' she said lightly.

'I'll see you tonight,' said Julius, in a voice which brooked no contradiction.

She made her escape, and spent the next hour or so wandering around the estate, incapable of coherent thought. No running away, he had said. She was tempted to check out of the hotel and go back to the farm, just to defy his orders. If he wanted to talk to her, why couldn't he talk on the telephone? But if she disappeared back to the farm, he would only follow her there. There was really nowhere she could run to. She would just have to face up to what he had to say, and deal with the humiliation later.

She left Mount Cotmayton and gained the privacy of her hotel room, where she soaked in a bath and then dressed in the navy basque skirt and white ruffled cotton shirt she had brought for dinner at the hotel. The outfit should fit the bill equally well for dinner with Julius, assuming he had dinner in mind. It was reasonably smart, with matching navy leather belt and court shoes. With her hair re-done in the chaotic topknot, she was pacing her room by a quarter to eight, trying to steel herself against the coming confrontation.

When she could stand the tension of waiting no longer, she snatched the navy jacket which matched the skirt, and opened her door ready to go down to the foyer, and then she gasped in surprise. Julius stood there, looking gaunt and tense, and she took a step backwards into the bedroom.

'I was just about to knock,' he said briefly, his eyes wary. He flicked his gaze over her, from her hair down to her navy court shoes, and then back up to rest intently on her face. She waited for him to say something else, then cleared her throat nervously when he stayed silent.

'Well, as you see, I'm ready. And I haven't run away. Are we going to eat, or stand here in the doorway all night?'

'We eat later,' Julius said, pushing past her into the bedroom, and closing the door carefully behind them. 'First, I've finally found the courage to give you some explanations, Victoria. And whether you like it or not, you're going to listen!'

CHAPTER NINE

VICTORIA backed away from him, alarmed by his air of determination. Her brain searched furiously for some kind of escape from the painful explanations Julius clearly felt he owed her. In a flash of inspiration, she said, 'Before this gets any heavier, Julius, let me just tell you I'm thinking of going to America. Sebastian might be offered a research post at the University of Southern California. He's asked me to go with him.'

'*What?*' His voice was soft but there was splintered glass in his tone.

'It would be a wrench leaving Roundbridge, of course,' she plunged on desperately. 'But I'll seriously think about it. It all really boils down to what's best for Charles.'

She stopped abruptly, because Julius caught hold of her in a furious lunge and pulled her hard against him, the iron rigidity of his muscles telling her how precariously he was controlling his temper.

She stayed quite still, stiff and resisting, but she was aware of his desire, transmitting itself like shock waves between them. The lidded gaze was achingly familiar. She had seen it before, and she knew what it meant. Her throat dried up in fear. Fear of her own weakness.

'There's no way you're going anywhere with Sebastian or with anyone else,' he said harshly, raking his fingers into her hair and discarding the band which held it up so that it tumbled round her face in wild confusion. 'You belong with me, you and Charles.'

The last words were groaned against her cheek, and then he found her mouth, and his tongue prised her lips apart and drove deeply inside in reckless possession, until it was

169

suddenly no use trying to resist the onslaught.

Hating herself, she still succumbed to the heat smouldering inside her and she began to kiss him back, mindlessly, in hungry despair, clutching frantically at his hair and stupidly trying to get closer although they were already moulded tightly together.

'Oh, Victoria . . . darling . . . ' He breathed her name like a caress, and with shuddering urgency he lifted her and laid her on the bed, pulling impatiently at the buttons on her blouse and skirt, the silver eyes burning with a need which melted her completely, emptying her brain of thought, fanning the flames in her stomach which were threatening to consume her.

'Damn you, Julius,' she whispered shakily. 'Oh, how I hate you.' But she was trembling all over, helpless with desire.

His mouth silenced her, and with the last of their clothes hurled anyhow on the floor Julius's hard body came against her softness, and with his hands and his lips arousing her to feverish impatience he thrust inside her, and they clung together in a shuddering explosion of passion which had left little time for preliminaries, and left Victoria shivering and exhausted in its aftermath.

After a long shattered silence, Julius levered himself away and rolled on to his back, still breathing rapidly, his eyes closed as if he were in agony.

And she knew how he felt. She was in agony too, an agony of remorse and self-disgust. Forcing herself to shake off the weakness and lethargy following their lovemaking, she swung her legs down and began to grab her clothes, pulling them on with trembling fingers, hating the tears which threatened to overflow and holding them back furiously.

When she had dressed, she turned on him coldly.

'You can go back to Susan now,' she said bleakly. 'Now you've proved what a great lover you still are!'

With a despairing groan, Julius slowly levered himself up, and began to shrug on his shirt, his lean hands shaking slightly as he struggled with the buttons. He stood up and dragged on his trousers, his eyes full of remorse as he watched her face.

'I'm sorry, Victoria—that wasn't premeditated. But when you talk about marrying another man, how do you expect me to react?'

'I expect you to congratulate me and wish me luck,' she grated bitterly. 'And who said anything about marriage? That's a fools' game.'

Julius stared at her bleakly, raising his hands and then dropping them by his sides, wearily.

'I'm sorry, I wish this hadn't happened.'

'I'm sure you do! Let's just hope I'm not quite as fertile as I was last time.' She loathed herself instantly she had said it, but it was too late to withdraw the words. Julius flinched, but his eyes didn't waver from her face.

'You don't understand. I'm sorry, because I came here to talk to you, try to explain the past.'

'I don't want to hear,' she retorted, her voice rising slightly. 'I don't want to know how responsible you feel, how sorry you feel for me, how . . . '

'Stop it! You're talking rubbish!' he said sharply, coming swiftly round the bed and pulling her down to sit beside him. 'Victoria, darling . . . I came to try to convince you how much I care for you! Goodness knows, I didn't mean to rush things like that, make you angry again!'

'I'm not angry. I just feel . . . humiliated,' she said unevenly.

'Then how can I make you understand? I'm not even sure where to begin.'

'Begin at the beginning,' she suggested carelessly. 'But you'll be wasting your breath. I understand you better than you think.'

He shook his head slowly. 'No, Victoria. You don't understand me at all. I'm no good at explaining my feelings. But I've never stopped wanting you, ever since that first weekend at the farm.'

'You expect me to believe that?' she exploded incredulously. 'I may be eleven years younger than you but

I'm not a simpleton! If you want someone you don't forget their existence for nearly two years!'

'But it's true,' he said quietly, a muscle working in his cheek. 'You've got to believe me.'

'I don't understand!'

'No, I'm not sure I do. There's no rational explanation for the effect you have on me.'

'You talk in riddles!' she shouted at him, raking her hair back from her face furiously. 'You say you actually cared for me, when we slept together that night, and yet you were so deliberately . . . so utterly hateful to me! And all this time, you've never contacted me . . .'

With a sudden, anguished groan Julius hunched forward, his elbows on his thighs, head in hands. She stared at his rigid figure, but bitterness kept her silent and motionless.

'All right,' he said finally, dropping his hands from his face, and easing back his broad shoulders slightly. 'I've told you, I'm no good at explaining my feelings. But I'll try. I looked at you, that day we first met, and you made a strong impact on me. I don't know what it was. What is it about someone else that draws you to them? Maybe it was the way you looked at me, with those tawny-almond eyes . . .'

He saw her cold face and spread his hands in a flat, despairing gesture. 'All I know is, I wanted you. And that frightened me. It still does. When I see someone I want that much I have this violent gut-reaction to block them out. I just want to fight the feeling any way I can.'

She sat rigid, listening but not understanding. Her hands were clenched tightly in her lap.

'So I put up some fairly heavy-duty barricades,' he went on with a trace of self-mockery in his eyes. 'But somehow you managed to get through. I told myself you were much too young. Virtually a child . . .'

'I was nearly nineteen,' she said sharply.

'Yes, but you were Hayley's younger sister, how could I seduce you under her roof? But you were looking at me as if I were blind, or half-witted or something! That was the hardest part of all. You wanted me, and you didn't even try to hide it. You were so vulnerable, innocent, sweet and generous, all the things I least wanted and least deserved. I just wanted to hit out, belittle you, devalue the whole thing.'

He shook his head wearily, his face drawn. 'When you came into my room that night, trying to explain how you felt, I finally snapped. I'll admit I took you for the wrong reasons. I thought if I took what you were offering, I'd somehow defuse the tension. Sex can be a very mechanical thing. I thought it might break the spell.' His mouth twisted in pain. 'Instead, I felt as if I'd jumped over a cliff into the dark.'

She closed her eyes tightly, then, and images of that night with Julius came swirling into her mind, mingling with the bitter ecstasy she had just experienced once more. The tenderness, the sheer, indescribable beauty of giving herself to Julius that first time, and the cruel slap in the face of his reaction afterwards. Her head was spinning. She was numbed by what Julius was trying to tell her. If his words were true, then he, too, had felt some of the magic of that weekend, he had sensed a deeper meaning to it all, shared something, just a fraction perhaps, of what she had experienced. It was a heady, potent possibility.

But if he had felt even a fraction of her consuming passion, he couldn't have left that night, and stayed away all that time. Without a word, or a letter, or even a phone call. It just wasn't possible. Her heart felt cold.

'New York seemed the perfect escape route,' he went on in a hunted voice, as if he was driving himself to continue. 'But I couldn't get you out of my mind. I painted a picture of you . . .' He gave a mirthless laugh, and she nodded slowly.

'Yes, I saw it at Hayley's.'

'I thought it might exorcise the ghosts. I'd transfer you to oil-paint and canvas and then get rid of you. Sell you, stick you in a cupboard, anything to get you out of my mind and give me some uninterrupted sleep at night!'

She met his eyes then, for the first time, staring at him curiously.

'And did you put me in a cupboard?'

'Yes, you were there for about a week. But it didn't work.' There was wry self-mockery in his voice again.

'Maybe you should have persevered with the therapy.'

'Yes, maybe.' Julius raked back his hair, and drew a deep breath. 'I tried quite a few others. Immersing myself in work, climbing and skiing at weekends.'

'Lots of other women?'

The lidded eyes glittered. 'No, no other women,' he said quietly. 'I made the acquaintance of several. But I took none of them to bed.'

'Ascetic as a monk,' she mocked faintly. 'I'd have thought the mechanical act of sex would have been just the thing to take your mind off things.'

'Yes, I thought so too. But after what I experienced with you, I found I felt differently about sex,' Julius said in a low, taut voice.

'How romantic!' she taunted, and he swung round to grip her shoulders, making her heart thump unevenly again.

'Don't do that!' he grated urgently. 'Knowing how much I've hurt you is bad enough. Seeing how much you've changed is even harder to bear. When we first met you were romantic, impulsive . . .'

'And now I'm calculating and cynical? Quite true. But what do you expect, Julius? Don't blame yourself!'

'Of course I blame myself!' he exclaimed, shaking her slightly. 'I should have written, or phoned, or come back and told you how I felt. I didn't. And by the time I knew what I really wanted I was so deeply embroiled in that mess over Sam Rochas I didn't even have time to think straight. And then I chose to resign, change the whole structure of my career. By that time messages, letters, phone calls—they would all have been worthless in trying to renew contact with you. I waited until I was back in England. I rang Hayley, and sounded her out. For all I knew you might have got married. When Hayley said you'd left university and taken up farming I knew something had to be wrong. You'd described your subject with so much dedication. Only a major disaster would have dragged you away from your studies. I gave the situation some thought, and then I came up with the only explanation.'

'Hayley said you guessed,' she agreed quietly, avoiding his eyes, staring at the tapestry pattern on the hotel bedspread. 'So you're saying Charles wasn't the only reason you looked me up again?' she asked finally, aware of an irritating tremble in her voice.

'I've just told you the truth, Victoria,' said Julius. 'I knew nothing about Charles until after I came back to find you. But finding out about him made me very angry. That wasn't logical, I know. You were under no obligation to tell me about the baby. But I felt angry with you, and with myself, and with the wasted months when I could have been with you, and with my baby son.'

She stared intently into space. She realised she was counting the pink and green flowers in the wallpaper border, interwoven in a twisted, heraldic design. Her sense of numbness grew, a sense of unreality, as if they were talking about two people completely unrelated to themselves.

'When we met again, you were so cool and distant, and different . . . all the things I'd been planning to say and do seemed impossible,' Julius was saying. 'I admit I'm useless at emotional scenes. I just want to run away as fast as I can in the opposite direction!'

'So what exactly do you want of me now, Julius?' she asked at last, turning a detached gaze on him.

'I want us to be together, Victoria! I want you and Charles and me to be a family. I want my son to know his father and his mother. I don't want him enduring the same deprivations I endured.

'But what makes you think we could provide a secure family unit for a child?' she persisted. 'I mean, from what you've just told me about your feelings, it's not exactly a glowing character reference for a stable family man, is it?'

The harsh face twisted into a wry smile.

'I can't answer that. All I know is, I want to be with you.

And with my son.'

'Yes, but barring sex, which I've just decided is a very poor basis for making decisions, what else do we have in common?'

He expelled his breath in a long, weary sigh, and stood up, pulling her slowly up to face him.

'Victoria, darling . . . sex might not be up to much as far as other people are concerned, but between you and me . . . ' The look in his eyes made her shiver with fresh panic and she steeled herself against him with every ounce of willpower she had left. 'Don't pretend there isn't magic, Victoria. And all we've had is one night, nearly two years ago. We won't count that hasty, rushed episode just now—that was extremely enjoyable but hardly did justice to the way I feel about you. You've no idea how much better it could be . . . ' He had moved a fraction closer, so gingerly she was taken by surprise when his lips brushed against her cheek, and his hands slid up into her hair. 'I want to make love to you very, very slowly . . .' he breathed against her ear, and with a slight strangled sob she found the impetus to push him violently away from her.

'Don't do that!' she said glacially. 'I can't think straight when you do that.'

Don't think, then. Just feel,' he murmured, a glitter of wry humour in his eyes.

'I want you to tell me what you think we have in common!' she demanded fiercely, clutching her arms around herself protectively. 'How do you see a relationship between us working? Because I'm afraid all I forecast is early failure. A father who gains his son's love, then walks away whenever responsibilities prove too demanding, is far worse than no father at all.'

The flash of humour faded, and Julius's voice sounded cooler, more distant when he at last spoke again.

'You're quite right. We should be practical and level-headed about this.' The grey eyes narrowed thoughtfully, 'What we need is a marriage contract, like the Elizabethans.'

'Marriage!' she bit out. 'Don't even bother suggesting it.

I'm not sure I could ever marry anyone. Let alone . . .'

'Let alone me?' he supplied, his jaw tensing. He looked suddenly bleaker, as if he sensed defeat. 'At least hear me out, Victoria! Apart from providing the missing parent for Charles, I could inject capital into Roundbridge, take some of the work-load off you, hire a full-time manager to run things. You would keep the farm in your own name, of course. I could keep the Knightsbridge house. We could go up to London for the theatre, and the ballet, and my business commitments.'

'And your charity auctions and dinners with Susan Goodman?' she cut in bitterly.

'Let's leave Susan, and for that matter Sebastian, out of this, shall we? We're discussing you and me,' he said coldly. 'We could split our time between the farm and city. I've got a place in Lombardy, near Lake Garda. We could put that in joint names, go there when I teach you and Charles to ski . . .'

'You have got it all worked out!' she burst out furiously.

Julius shrugged. 'I've had nearly two years to think about it,' he pointed out with justice. 'As far as common interests go, I've been working on an outline for a book recently, on the art treasures of the world. The royalties are going to the NSPCC.'

'More conscience-salving,' she murmured, but Julius ignored her.

'I thought maybe you'd like to help me with it—with your love of history and my knowledge of antiques we might prove a good team.' He hesitated a moment, and then smiled slightly, some of his icy control disappearing. 'And then, let's see, you could maybe sign an undertaking to accompany me rock-climbing, and skiing, and promise to eat the vegetarian meals I cook for you, and I could undertake to come swimming and dancing with you, and take you to see Shakespeare, and buy you Italian meals, and boxes of chocolates . . .'

'Oh, stop it, please!' she broke in, shaking her head and

covering her ears with her hands, feeling a mixture of hysterical amusement and despair. 'I can't take all this in. I can't think. I can't even tell you what I feel right now.'

'Victoria.' His deep voice was a caress, with a vibration which touched a dangerous chord deep inside her. 'Please, my love, forgive me. Say you forgive me. Let me try to put things right between us.'

'That's just it,' she whispered painfully, turning away. 'That's the worst thing. I honestly don't think you ever can.'

'Don't say that!' Julius's voice was low, with a slight break in it which made her jerk up her head and stare at him in anguish. For a dreadful moment she thought he was crying. There was a muscle working spasmodically in his lean cheek, and the silver eyes were suspiciously brilliant beneath the lowered lids. She felt as if she was splintering into a thousand fragments.

'Darling, let me take you back to bed again, now,' he said huskily, the words barely audible in the hush of the room. 'Let me make love to you again, and show you what I really feel for you.'

'No!' She was near hysteria, putting up her arms in a defensive jerk and backing away. 'Please, just leave me alone, Julius. I just can't face all the heartache again! Oh, Julius, I loved you so much! You'll never know how much! It was so instant, so overwhelming, there was nothing I could do about it. I felt as if we were supposed to be together, as if I'd known you before, somehow. For six months after you went to New York I waited and waited. I was so sure you'd realise you'd been wrong, and find you couldn't live without me after all . . .'

'I did,' he said gently, his face tense and bleak as he stared at her.

'But it's too late!' she said brokenly. 'When you didn't come back, I knew I had to stop thinking about you, stop loving you. I had to make myself stop caring! If I hadn't, I could never have carried on with my life.'

'I love you, Victoria,' he said simply, the grey eyes dark

with pain.

'Then if you really love me, leave me in peace!' she sobbed desperately, turning her back on him and covering her face with her hands.

'Is that really what you want?' His voice sounded strange, hoarser.

'Oh, just go away! Just go, Julius!'

She stood rigidly, with her back to him, and after what seemed an eternity she heard the door softly open and close, and she realised Julius had really gone.

She swung round and stared around the empty bedroom, then sank on to the bed, completely enervated. She couldn't think. Her brain felt deadened. She had no idea how much time elapsed before she stiffly began to pack her case, and checked out of the hotel. All she knew was an awful sinking emptiness inside, and the need to get home, back to the timeless security of Roundbridge, to gather her shattered thoughts together.

CHAPTER TEN

'VICKY! You're back early! Didn't you see anything at the auction?' Hayley's brown eyes were anxious when Victoria called to collect Charles early next morning. With an encompassing glance at her white face and stricken expression, Hayley caught Victoria's hands and pulled her quickly into the warmth of the hall.

'Good grief, you're frozen! Come into Andrew's study and sit by the fire. Tell me what's happened, Vicky! What's wrong?'

'Everything's wrong,' said Victoria wearily, meeting Hayley's eyes with a travesty of a grin. 'I've been really stupid this time, Hayley.'

Tears threatened to choke her, and her sister hugged her tightly.

'How did you get so *cold*, Vicky? What *have* you been doing?'

'Driving round,' she confessed, with a short laugh. 'Since I left the hotel last night. I wanted time to think. I parked up on the Burton Hills and . . . '

'All *night?*'

She nodded, vaguely registering Hayley's appalled expression.

'Vicky, I know you're an impulsive idiot, but what possessed you to do such a thing?' Hayley was propelling her into the leather armchair by the fire as she scolded, and calling to Andrew to bring a cup of tea. 'Thank goodness it didn't freeze last night, that's all. You could have died of hypothermia, you idiot!'

Victoria gratefully accepted the tea which Andrew brought in, and stared bleakly at Hayley after he had tactfully

180

withdrawn again.

'Everything's a hopeless mess,' she said at last, shivering as the hot liquid thawed her slightly. 'I told Julius to go away . . . I told him I didn't love him.'

She stopped abruptly, pressing her fingers to her mouth, grappling for control, and then in a garbled rush the whole disastrous confrontation came pouring out, in bitter, jerky sentences, while Hayley sat silently, shaking her head in despair.

'Has Julius gone back to London, do you think?' she asked, when Victoria had finished her tale.

'I don't know,' Victoria admitted, miserably, blowing her nose on a tissue and sipping a second cup of tea.

'Victoria, was it true? Do you *really* want Julius to stay away from you and Charles?'

She raised hunted eyes to her sister's gaze, and then shook her head jerkily.

'No . . . no!' she groaned, rubbing her forehead wearily. 'I love him! So much it terrifies me. I just felt . . . I felt I couldn't face it all over again. I thought, how can I explain? I'm not even sure how to explain it to myself!'

'You're frightened of being vulnerable again?' Hayley suggested softly. 'Afraid to trust him?'

Victoria sighed shakily. 'Yes, partly. And I've been having a bit of a struggle with my pride.'

Hayley laughed gently. 'I wonder why?' she teased. 'Surely you're not about to admit you're as proud and stubborn as a mule?'

'Are mules proud? I thought that was peacocks,' she countered, smiling reluctantly.

'No, peacocks are vain, and that's one vice you definitely don't have, my love.'

Hayley poured the last cup of tea into Victoria's cup, and sat back with a thoughtful gleam in her eyes which was all too familiar.

'Don't tell me you've another brilliant plan,' Victoria sighed, with a trace of sarcasm. 'You've stuck your oar in enough already!'

'That's a very inelegant expression,' retorted Hayley calmly, sounding just like their mother. 'And all I've been doing is try and push together two of the nicest and stupidest people I know!'

Victoria managed a smile, but her heart felt leaden. Her cold vigil, huddled in the Range Rover last night, had seemed to open a window on a dazzling, painfully bright truth. Julius had summoned every ounce of courage to beg her forgiveness. He had said he was no good at grovelling, but he had made a pretty good job of it. And she had sent him away. He had said he loved her, and she had been too strangled with fear and pride to accept it.

'I thought he was in love with Susan Goodman,' she told Hayley suddenly, her voice distracted. 'But he wasn't.'

'Of course he wasn't,' Hayley agreed patiently. 'She's been in love with him for years, but you know how good Julius is at keeping people at arm's length.'

'Yes.' She lowered her eyes, remembering their frantic, explosive lovemaking last night. She had somehow got through his barricades, he had said. All that intense, repressed passion appeared to be for her alone. Last night's sensations flooded back through her, and she blushed involuntarily, warmth gradually displacing the chill inside her.

Hayley was watching her, her expression so anxious Victoria smiled, reassuringly, and stood up.

'I'm all right now. Thanks for the tea and sympathy. How's Charles?'

'Blooming. Currently plastering Weetabix all over Elspeth and the kitchen floor, since you ask!'

'Oh dear, sorry.' She went to investigate, Hayley following, and the sight of her son, happily coated in breakfast cereal, beaming at the equally disreputable faces of his two infant cousins, seemed finally to put everything into perspective. Uncaring of his sticky state, she lifted Charles out of his high chair and cuddled him close against her.

'I'll take him home now,' she told Hayley, as Elspeth

began to collect all the paraphernalia of nappies and toys which accompanied him.

'No, wait.' Hayley caught her arm. 'Ring Julius, darling. Let him know how you feel, before it's too late.'

Victoria eyed the telephone in the hall with conflicting emotions.

'I'm not sure what I could say on the phone,' she said, slowly, standing irresolute for a moment. Then a sudden flash of inspiration came to her, and she looked pleadingly at Hayley and Elspeth.

'Can you look after Charles for me today? I'd like to drive up to London, surprise him . . . '

'Of course we will, but darling, are you sure you're up to driving all that way? You look more in need of a good breakfast and a decent night's sleep. Ring him! He'd come like a shot, I know he would.'

'No. It's important that I go to him this time,' she said with conviction. 'I must go and see him today.'

The last cold traces of doubt were melting inside her, like ice in spring sunshine. With Hayley's admonitions to drive carefully ringing in her ears, she stopped first at the farm to shower and change, and as an impulsive afterthought she returned to her room and sprayed herself liberally with her atomiser of Anaïs Anaïs, which had gathered dust on her dressing-table for nearly two years. It seemed to be a significant gesture.

Then, fragantly elegant in her straw silk coat-dress and cream jacket, she was speeding south down the motorway, her tiredness forgotten in the rush of adrenalin coursing through her.

Two hours later she was rapping on the front door of Campion House, with the heavy brass knocker. Sansom was in his usual position in the daffodil barrel, she realised, smiling involuntarily at the flattened patch of flowers and the unrepentant contentment on the cat's face.

The door opened and with a jolt she found herself facing Susan Goodman's polite smile of enquiry.

'Oh, hello. You didn't want to see Julius, did you?'

Victoria smiled back politely, her throat dry.

'Yes. Is he there?'

'No, he's gone to Milan. Didn't he tell you?'

Victoria felt her stomach tying itself into a dozen knots. 'To Milan? Are you quite sure?'

'Quite sure. Do you want to come and search the house?'

Victoria flushed. 'Do you mind telling me what you're doing here, if Julius is away?'

'Sorting out last-minute arrangements with his housekeeper,' said Susan, narrowing her eyes curiously on Victoria's distraught face. 'He left rather on the spur of the moment. He's not sure when he's coming back—he could be away for months. So he wanted to be sure Sansom gets fed, and the house gets aired, you know.'

Victoria stared at the other girl in blank confusion. Julius had gone. Without telling her. There was a pain inside which refused to go away, and an inner voice was saying 'Why not? You told him to go away. He's gone.' A sudden thought came to her, a faint ray of hope.

'When was his flight? Can you tell me, please?'

Susan frowned, and went to find a large organiser bag, extracting a diary and flicking through the pages with nerve-shattering slowness. 'Let's see . . . yes, it's an Alitalia flight from Heathrow. AZ 459, leaving 10.55 a.m. from Terminal Two.' She looked up, eyebrows raised, adding, 'It's half-past ten already. I'm afraid it's much too late to catch him. I've got his address and phone number for his place on Lake Garda. I'll pass a message on if you like.'

Victoria wasn't listening, she was half-way down the steps already and running towards the car, frantically thinking about the quickest way to Heathrow from Knightsbridge. Please God, the flight might be delayed, there might be engine trouble, there might be a baggage handlers' strike, anything, anything . . .

With shaking fingers she flipped through the London *A to Z* in the glovebox, flinging it on to the floor when she realised the airport fell just outside the area covered by the atlas. Making a quick logical decision she continued westwards along Knightsbridge and took the A4, feeling sure it went in the right direction. It was a nightmare drive. Traffic lights, hold-ups, road-works, everything imaginable seemed to have been placed deliberately to hinder her progress. She turned on the radio to hear the time-checks, but the disc jockey's inane babble was unbearable in her present state of tension.

She switched off and concentrated on avoiding obstacles with gritted teeth and pounding heart, until she thought the stress was going to kill her.

By the time she reached the airport, it was long past take-off time. Braking jerkily by the main entrance doors, she ignored the indignant shout of a taxi driver and left the Range Rover there as she ran into the terminal, frantically searching for the Alitalia desk. She reached it with the blood pounding dizzily in her ears, and her breathing ragged.

'Flight AZ 459 to Milan?' The clerk repeating her enquiry was Italian, with olive skin and sleek, dark hair, and it seemed to Victoria that she was feigning a deliberate lack of urgency. 'Yes, I think they've just boarded. There was a short delay. The flight takes off in one minute.'

'Are you sure?'

The girl looked offended. 'Of course I am sure.' said haughtily.

Victoria sank back against the desk, feeling sick, light-headed and horribly empty. She had had no dinner last night, no sleep, and no breakfast this morning, it suddenly dawned on her. As the adrenalin trickled out of her system exhaustion hit her like a tidal wave. She was dimly aware that the Italian clerk was staring at her curiously, but the crowds around her seemed to be surging and receding in a sickening way, and to her intense horror she watched the floor rushing up to meet her before she fainted.

In what seemed only a matter of seconds, she was staring blankly at a circle of feet and legs, the centre of a babble of concerned exclamations and helping hands. She pushed herself up on one elbow, trying to gather her wits, but then, when a deep, achingly familiar voice demanded to be allowed through the crowd, she feared she was concussed, hallucinating, because it couldn't possibly be Julius, scattering people right and left, bending over her and lifting her gently to her feet.

'Julius?'

'I don't believe it!' he said harshly, frowning at her incredulously. 'Victoria! What the hell are you doing here?'

'Looking for you,' she said shakily, swaying into his arms. Julius stiffened, supporting her but not holding her tightly the way she wanted him to. 'Your secretary said you'd gone to Milan. You can't be here, because your flight's just taken off.' She wasn't quite sure if she was making sense.

'I decided not to get on it,' Julius said flatly, his dark face expressionless. 'I was on my way back here to Alitalia to discuss getting my luggage back when I saw you lying on the floor surrounded by an audience.' Glancing round them they realised that among the steady flow of arrivals and departures, they were still being observed by a small, interested group of spectators.

'What happened to you? Did you faint?' he asked curtly, his pale eyes intent on her face. 'You're as white as a sheet.'

She nodded. 'My fault—lack of food and lack of sleep. Julius, why aren't you on your plane to Milan?'

'Because I couldn't go,' he said quietly. 'I'd have been running away again. I swore I'd stop that. And I've discovered a strong masochistic streak in myself since I met you, Victoria.'

She gazed up into his face, seeing how tense and weary he looked. Had he lost weight? Maybe he had been skipping meals, too.

'Why were you following me?' he asked, suddenly harsher. 'Is something wrong?'

'I love you,' she whispered, simply. 'I had to tell you.'

She was only dimly aware of the delighted intake of breath from the avid onlookers.

But Julius didn't move. He seemed turned to stone, completely dumbfounded. Eventually he said softly, 'Say it again.' There was a pulse beating erratically in his lean cheek.

'I love you.'

Another painful silence, but she could see a dark tinge of colour along his cheekbones, and the silver eyes seemed to devour her, hungrily travelling over her from head to toe, and as the stunned silence lengthened she began to tremble weakly.

'You've put me through hell,' he muttered at last, his voice rough, but then he lifted a shaking hand to trace the line of her cheek slowly, wonderingly, as if he were trying to convince himself that she really existed. 'But you know that, don't you?'

She nodded blindly. 'I'm sorry, Julius.'

'No, maybe it serves me right,' he murmured, jerking her suddenly against him and holding her in a crushing embrace which knocked her breath away. 'That's just what I've done to you, all these months.' His hand was holding her head tightly against his chest, and she could hear the rapid pounding of his heart. Blissfully she wrapped her arms round him, feeling the hard ridges of his back muscles through the supple suede jacket. She felt idiotically, ludicrously happy. She had no idea how long they stood there, locked together, uncaring of their audience. But eventually Julius smiled down into her face, a rueful gleam in his eyes.

'I'll ring the airline later about my luggage,' he smiled. 'But this seems to be a very public place for very private feelings.' He kissed the top of her head lightly, and steered her away from the intrigued Alitalia staff and the small group of adolescent schoolgirls who were gazing misty-eyed at Julius, and lingering to see what happened next.

'I think they were hoping you'd kiss me,' she laughed shakily, as Julius took the Range Rover keys from her and ushered her firmly into the passenger seat.

'But kissing you is definitely something to do in private,' said Julius, the lidded eyes melting her bones as he smiled at her. 'One thing invariably leads to another with you, in my experience.'

She smiled radiantly at him, leaning her head back on the seat-rest and letting her eyelids droop. Her sleepless night caught abruptly up with her, and when she opened her eyes she was shocked to see they had stopped outside the Knightsbridge house.

'Time to wake up,' said Julius softly, helping her out. 'I've a feeling this situation calls for champagne, my darling, but frankly, looking at you, all I can think of is a high-protein breakfast and eight hours' sleep.'

She allowed herself to be led to a chair in the white-tiled kitchen, and leant her chin on her elbows while Julius conducted a lightning search of the freezer.

'Bacon and eggs?' he asked over his shoulder. She nodded contentedly.

'Wonderful.'

The microwave produced three rashers of bacon and two poached eggs each in record time, and they ate ravenously and silently, Julius's eyes rarely leaving her face, and her pulses beginning to respond in spite of her weariness.

'Feeling better?' he asked softly, as he handed her a steaming cup of coffee.

'Almost back to normal,' she smiled.

'Do I gather you didn't go to bed last night?' he asked finally, his light eyes probing on her face.

'No, I have to confess I didn't.'

'So what did you do, Victoria?'

'I intended to drive back to the farm. But instead I ended up parked on Burton Hills, like a zombie, until the sun came up. I've never actually watched the sun rise before. Not all of it. It's breathtaking. Like a revelation. I think that was the moment I finally knew what a fool I'd been.'

'Then thank goodness for the sunrise,' said Julius huskily, leaning over to kiss her lingeringly on the mouth. The kiss conveyed more than words. When she raised her head and gazed into his eyes, she felt as if she were drowning.

'So what did *you* do?' she whispered, reaching out for his hand and holding it tightly between both of hers.

'I drove back here.' Julius gave a twisted smile. 'And I drank quite a lot of malt whisky. And I came to the conclusion that if I was hurting you so much by being around, maybe I should disappear again. Leave you in peace. And that if Sebastian could make you happy maybe I'd better let him . . .'

'I never even considered going to America with him,' she confessed guiltily. 'I said it to protect myself. I was terrified of what you were going to say, hearing your excuses, seeing your pity.'

He tightened his grasp of her hands, and she leaned closer, finding it impossible to get close enough while sitting on her chair and climbing on to his knee, putting her arms round his neck and sliding her fingers into his hair.

'The idea that another man . . . that you'd let him make love to you,' he groaned against her cheek. 'It was like refined torture.'

'I've never slept with Sebastian,' she told him softly. 'The only man I've ever . . . had sex with?' She smiled with a touch of teasing in her eyes. 'Or should I call it made love with, is you!'

'From now on we call it making love,' said Julius hoarsely, crushing her against him, and she nodded, tracing her fingers along the strong column of his neck, and trying to suppress the urge to sing and cry with happiness.

'I thought you loved Susan Goodman,' she went on. 'But you definitely don't, do you?'

'No, I definitely don't,' he agreed. 'When did you dream that up?'

'Remember that day we took Charles to the park? You said that up till eighteen months ago, you'd never met anyone you wanted to get involved with. I thought you couldn't possibly be talking about me. So you meant you'd fallen in love with someone else. Just before that weekend at Hayley's. And that you'd had to put up with my infatuation with you, while you were in love with someone else.'

'So that's why you froze on me,' Julius said slowly, cupping her face in his hands and searching her face intensely, as if he was trying to memorise every feature. 'How could I possibly love anyone else, after seeing you, balanced upside-down on your hands and then collapsing flat on your back at my feet!'

She giggled. 'True. I see what you mean now.'

'Have I told you how beautiful you are?' He smiled into her face.

'No, I don't believe you ever have.' There was warmth creeping up her neck at the expression in the lidded gaze, and she pressed closer to him, suffused with desire and suddenly unaccountably shy. 'Oh, Julius,' she whispered against his chest, 'I was so ashamed of myself, last night, after you left . . . I felt so cold and spiteful and mean.'

'Three things you could never be,' he murmured, his hands sliding hungrily over her soft curves beneath the silk dress. 'You're the warmest, most generous, most impulsive woman I've ever been privileged to meet.'

'Hayley said I was impulsive,' she said softly, catching her breath as his caress became unmistakably sexual, and her body writhed towards him involuntarily. 'But I haven't been over the last eighteen months. Having a baby has made me much more . . . disciplined, somehow. I've felt I've been calculating every move, weighing everything up like some cautious old maid.' She looked into his face, trying to explain herself. 'I think having Charles has given me more confidence, though. You have to rely on your own instincts with a baby.'

'You've done a brilliant job,' Julius told her warmly. 'But I think today proves you're back to normal, my love!' He gave a low laugh. 'Staying awake all night watching the sun rise, then driving a hundred miles on an empty stomach seems more like the old you! Plus your crazy dash to the airport. You didn't have a hope in hell of catching me if I'd got on that plane.'

'It was delayed,' she argued with justice, 'and if you had gone, I'd only have missed you by a few minutes!'

He was laughing at her, and she stared at him hungrily, ensnared by his devastating smile and revelling in the dawning knowledge that she no longer had to hide its effect on her.

'Take me to bed,' she whispered simply, and Julius nodded gravely, deliberately misunderstanding her.

'Straight away. You look exhausted. Sleep is just what you need.'

'Sleep was the last thing I had in mind,' she remonstrated, blushing as he swept her up into his arms and began to carry her upstairs. 'Don't tease me, Julius.'

'I've no intention of teasing you, my darling,' he said huskily, laying her on his bed and looking down at her with an expression which turned her bones to water. 'I intend to keep my promise . . . '

He was unbuttoning the silk dress with a hint of impatience, and she laughed shakily up at him.

'What promise was that?'

'The promise I made last night. To make love to you very, very, very slowly . . . '

His smile was dazzling as he bent to kiss her, and with a shock of happiness she smiled back at him, the shadows of the past vanishing completely as she opened her arms to the man she loved.

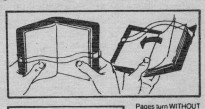